Jonah gritted out, 'I'm trying to rescue you, which will not be possible unless you stop struggling.'

The woman stopped wriggling long enough to shoot him a flat stare. 'I'm an excellent swimmer,' she croaked. 'I swam conference for Bryn Mawr.'

Not just a tourist, Jonah thought, with her posh American accent ringing in his ears. *From the whole other side of the world.*

'Could have fooled me,' he muttered. 'Unless that's what passes for the Australian Crawl Stateside these days.'

The stare became a glare. And her eyes... A wicked green, they were, only one was marred with a whopping great splotch of brown.

And while *he* stared *her* hand slipped. Luckily she had the smarts to grab the pointy end of his board, leaving him to clench his thighs for all he was worth.

'Honey,' he growled, by then near the end of his limited patience, 'I understand that you're embarrassed. 'But would you rather be humbled or dead?'

Her strange eyes flinted at the *honey*—not that he gave a damn. All he cared was that she gave a short nod. The sooner he dumped her back on the sand and got on with his day the better. And if a dose of reality was necessary to get it done, then so be it.

Dear Reader

Far North Queensland is a beautiful part of the world—and only a hop, skip and a short plane ride from where I live. The beaches are magnificent, the sun is hot, and the skies are endless. And what with all that gorgeousness and sultry heat, the flash resorts and the great bars and cafés—well, the possibility of a hot summer romance is ripe.

From all that my hero, Jonah North, was born. Strong and taciturn. All sun-drenched skin, quicksilver eyes, brawn, candour and capability. A man with a wild past that has him shouldering regret, and a rare smile that'll melt your knees from ten paces. He's a *bloke*. A man's man. And one the ladies like quite a bit as well—myself included! All I had to do was throw him the most unlikely heroine—cool, unimpressed, desperately independent and a tourist—then sit back and watch as the sparks flew and the mighty tree was felled.

I hope you enjoy the show as much as I did!

Till then, happy reading. And keep a fan on hand—when Jonah hits the page you might need it! :)

Ally

www.allyblake.com

Those Summer Nights
In Crescent Cove find sun, sea and steamy nights…

This hot, sultry duet continues next month with
THE HEAT OF THE NIGHT by Amy Andrews.
Don't miss Claudia's story!

HER HOTTEST SUMMER YET

BY
ALLY BLAKE

First published in Great Britain 2014
by Mills & Boon, an imprint of Harlequin (UK) Limited,
Eton House, 18-24 Paradise Road, Richmond, Surrey, TW9 1SR

© 2014 Ally Blake

ISBN: 978 0 263 24258 4

Harlequin (UK) Limited's policy is to use papers that are natural,
renewable and recyclable products and made from wood grown in
sustainable forests. The logging and manufacturing processes conform
to the legal environmental regulations of the country of origin.

Printed and bound in Great Britain
by CPI Antony Rowe, Chippenham, Wiltshire

B000 000 012 2112

In her previous life Australian author **Ally Blake** was at times a cheerleader, a maths tutor, a dental assistant and a shop assistant. In this life she is a bestselling, multi-award-winning novelist who has been published in over twenty languages with more than two million books sold worldwide.

She married her gorgeous husband in Las Vegas—no Elvis in sight, though Tony Curtis did put in a special appearance—and now Ally and her family, including three rambunctious toddlers, share a property in the leafy western suburbs of Brisbane, with kookaburras, cockatoos, rainbow lorikeets and the occasional creepy-crawly. When not writing, she makes coffees that never get drunk, eats too many M&Ms, attempts yoga, devours *The West Wing* reruns, reads every spare minute she can and barracks ardently for the Collingwood Magpies footy team.

You can find out more at her website, www.allyblake.com

Other Modern Tempted™ titles by Ally Blake:

THE DANCE OFF
FAKING IT TO MAKING IT

This and other titles by Ally Blake are available in eBook format from www.millsandboon.co.uk

This one is for all the long, hot Australian summers of my life; for all the memories and possibilities they hold.

With an extra dollop of love for Amy Andrews, one of my favourite writers and a sublime woman to boot.

CHAPTER ONE

AVERY SHAW BARELY noticed the salty breeze whipping pale blonde hair across her face and fluttering the diaphanous layers of her dress against her legs. She was blissfully deep in a whirlpool of warm, hazy, happy memories as she stood on the sandy footpath and beamed up at the facade of the Tropicana Nights Resort.

She lifted a hand to shield her eyes from the shimmering Australian summer sun, and breathed the place in. It was bigger than she remembered, and more striking. Like some great white colonial palace, uprooted out of another era and transplanted to the pretty beach strip that was Crescent Cove. The garden now teetered on the wild side, and its facade was more than a little shabby around the edges. But ten years did that to a place.

Things changed. She was hardly the naive sixteen-year-old with the knobbly knees she'd been the summer she was last there. Back when all that mattered was friends, and fun, and—

A loud whoosh and rattle behind her tugged Avery back to the present. She glanced down the curving sidewalk to see a group of skinny brown-skinned boys in board shorts hurtling across the road on their skateboards before running down the beach and straight into the sparkling blue water of the Pacific.

And sometimes, she thought with a pleasant tightening in her lungs, *things don't change much at all*.

Lungs full to bursting with the taste of salt and sea and expectation, Avery and her Vuitton luggage set bumped merrily up the wide front steps and into the lobby. Huge faux marble columns held up the two-storey ceiling. Below sat cushy lounge chairs, colossal rugs, and potted palms dotted a floor made of the most beautiful swirling mosaic tiles in a million sandy tones. And by the archway leading to the restaurant beyond sat an old-fashioned noticeboard shouting out: Two-For-One Main Courses at the Capricorn Café For Any Guests Sporting an Eye Patch!

She laughed, the sound bouncing about in the empty space. For the lobby was empty, which for a beach resort at the height of summer seemed odd. But everyone was probably at the pool. Or having siestas in their rooms. And considering the hustle and bustle Avery had left behind in Manhattan, it was a relief.

Deeper inside the colossal entrance, reception loomed by way of a long sandstone desk with waves carved into the side. Behind said desk stood a young woman with deep red hair pulled back into a long sleek ponytail, her name tag sporting the Tropicana Nights logo slightly askew on the jacket of the faded yellow and blue Hawaiian print dress, which might well have been worn in the seventies.

"Ahoy, there!" sing-songed the woman—whose name tag read Isis—front teeth overlapping endearingly. Then, seeing Avery's gaze light upon the stuffed parrot wiggling on her shoulder, Isis gave the thing a scratch under the chin. "It's Pirates and Parrots theme at the resort this week."

"Of course it is," Avery said, the eye patch now making more sense. "I'm Avery Shaw. Claudia Davis is expecting me."

"Yo ho ho, and a bottle of rum… The American!"

"That I am!" The girl's pep was infectious, jet lag or no.

"Claude has been beside herself all morning, making me check the Qantas website hourly to make sure you arrived safe and sound."

"That's my girl," Avery said, feeling better and better about her last-minute decision to fly across the world, to the only person in her world who'd understand why.

Tap-tap-tap went Isis's long aqua fingernails on the keyboard. "Now, Claude could be…anywhere. Things have been slightly crazy around here since her parents choofed off."

Choofed off? Maybe that was Aussie for *retired*. Crazy or not, when Avery had first called Claude to say she was coming, Claude had sounded giddy that the management of the resort her family had owned for the past twenty years was finally up to her. She had ideas! Brilliant ones! People were going to flock as they hadn't flocked in years!

Glancing back at the still-empty lobby, Avery figured the *flocking* was still in the planning. "Shall I wait?"

"*No* ho ho," said Isis, back to tapping at the keyboard, "you'll be waiting till next millennium. Get thee to thy room. Goodies await. I'll get one of the crew to show you the way."

Avery glanced over her shoulder, her mind going instantly to the stream of messages her friends had sent when they'd heard she was heading to Australia, most of which were vividly imagined snippets of advice on how best to lure a hot, musclebound young porter "down under."

The kid ambling her way *was* young—couldn't have been a day over seventeen. But with his bright red hair and galaxy of freckles, hunching over his lurid yellow and blue shirt and wearing a floppy black pirate hat that had seen better days, he probably wasn't what they'd had in mind.

"Cyrus," Isis said, an impressive warning note creeping into her voice.

Cyrus looked up, his flapping sandshoes coming to a slow halt. Then he grinned, the overlapping teeth putting it beyond doubt that he and Isis were related.

"This is Miss Shaw," warned Isis. "Claudia's friend."

"Thanks, Cyrus," Avery said, heaving her luggage onto the golden trolley by the desk since Cyrus was too busy staring to seem to remember how.

"Impshi," Isis growled. "Kindly escort Miss Shaw to the Tiki Suite."

Avery's bags wobbled precariously as Cyrus finally grabbed the high bar of the trolley and began loping off towards the rear of the lobby.

"You're the New Yorker," he said.

Jogging to catch up, Avery said, "I'm the New Yorker."

"So how do *you* know Claude anyway? She never goes *anywhere*," said Cyrus, stopping short and throwing out an arm that nearly got her around the neck. She realised belatedly he was letting a couple of women with matching silver hair and eye-popping orange sarongs squeeze past.

Avery ducked under Cyrus's arm. "Claude has been all over the place, and I know because I went with her. The best trips were Italy…Morocco… One particular night in the Maldives was particularly memorable. We first met when my family holidayed here about ten years back."

Not *about* ten years. *Exactly.* Nearly to the day. There'd be no forgetting that these next few weeks. No matter how far from home she was.

"Now, come on Cyrus," Avery said, shaking off the sudden weight upon her chest. She looped a hand through the crook of Cyrus's bony elbow and dragged him in the direction of her suite. "Take me to my room."

Kid nearly tripped over his size thirteens.

One wrong turn and a generous tip later the Tiki Suite was all hers, and Avery was alone in the blissful cool of the soft, worn, white-on-white decor where indeed goodies did await: a basket of warm-skinned peaches, plums and nectarines, a box of divine chocolate, and a huge bottle of pink bubbly.

But first Avery kicked off her shoes and moved to the French doors, where the scent of sea air and the lemon trees that bordered the wall of her private courtyard filled her senses. She lifted her face to the sun to find it hotter than back home, crisper somehow.

It was the same suite in which her family had stayed a decade before. Her mother had kicked up a fuss when they'd discovered the place was less glamorous than she'd envisaged, but by that stage Avery had already met Claude and begged to stay. For once her dear dad had put his foot down, and Avery had gone on to have a magical, memorable, lazy, hazy summer.

The last simple, wonderful, innocent summer of her life.

The last before her parents' divorce.

The divorce her mother was about to celebrate with a Divorced a Decade party, in fact; capitals intended.

Avery glanced over her shoulder at the tote she'd left on the bed, and tickles of perspiration burst over her skin.

She had to call home, let her mother know she'd arrived. Even though she knew she'd barely get in a hello before she was force fed every new detail of the big bash colour theme—*blood*-red—guest lists—exclusive yet extensive—and all-male live entertainment—no, *no*, NO!

Avery sent a text.

I'm here! Sun is shining. Beach looks splendiferous. I'll call once jet lag wears off. Prepare yourself for stories of backyard tattoos, pub crawls, killer spiders the size of a studio apartment, and naked midnight beach sprints. Happy to hear the same from you. Ave xXx

Then, switching off her phone, she threw it to the bed. Then shoved a pillow over the top.

Knowing she couldn't be trusted to sit in the room and wait for Claude without turning her phone back on, Avery changed into a swimsuit, lathered suncreen over every exposed inch, grabbed a beach towel, and headed out to marvel at the Pacific.

As she padded through the resort, smiling at each and every one of Claude's—yes, Claude's!—pink-faced guests, Avery thought about how her decision to come back had been purely reactive, a panic-driven emotional hiccup when her mother had broached the idea of the Divorced a Decade party for the very first time.

But now she was here, the swirl of warm memories seeping under her skin, she wondered why it had never occurred to her sooner to come back. To come full circle.

Because that's how it felt. Like over the next few weeks she'd not only hang with her bestie—or nab herself a willing cabana boy to help get the kinks out—but maybe even be able to work her way back to how things had been here before her family had flown back to Manhattan and everything had fallen apart. To find the hopeful girl she'd once been before her life had become an endless series of gymnastic spins from one parent to the other and back again. Cartwheels to get her absent father's attention. Cheerleading her way through her mother's wild moods.

She'd never felt quite as safe, as secure, as *content* since that summer.

The summer of her first beer.

Her first beach bonfire.

Her first crush…

Avery's feet came to a squeaking halt.

In fact, wasn't *he*—the object of said crush—in Crescent Cove, right now?

Claude had mentioned him. Okay, so she'd bitched and

moaned; that he was *only* in the cove till he and Claudia
sorted out what they were going to do with the resort now
that their respective parents had retired and left the two of
them in charge. But that was about *Claude's* history with
the guy, not Avery's.

Her history was nice. And at that moment *he* was there.
And *she* was there. It would be nice to look him up. And
compared to the supercharged emotional tornado that was
her family life in New York, this summer Avery could really do with some *nice*.

Jonah North pushed his arms through the rippling water,
the ocean cool sliding over the heat-baked skin of his back
and shoulders, his feet trailing lazily through the water
behind him.

Once he hit a sweet spot—calm, warm, a good distance
from the sand—he pressed himself to sitting, legs either
side of his board. He ran two hands over his face, shook
the water from his hair, and took in the view.

The town of Crescent Cove was nestled behind a double row of palm trees that fringed the curved beach that
gave the place its name. Through the gaps were flashes
of pastel—huge resorts, holiday accommodation, locally
run shops, as well as scattered homes of locals yet to sell
out. Above him only sky, behind and below the endless
blue of the Pacific. Paradise.

It was late in the morning for a paddle—there'd been
no question of carving out enough time to head down the
coast where coral didn't hamper actual surf. Who was he
kidding? There was never any time. Which, for a lobsterman's son, whose sea legs had come in before his land
legs, was near sacrilege.

But he was here now.

Jonah closed his eyes, tilted his face to the sun, soaked
in its life force. No sound to be heard bar the heave of his

slowing breaths, the gentle lap of water against his thighs, a scream—

His eyes snapped open, his last breath trapped in his lungs. His ears strained. His gaze sweeping the gentle rolling water between himself and the sand, searching for—

There. A keening. Not a gull. Not music drifting on the breeze from one of the resort hotels. Distress. Human distress.

Muscles seized, every sense on red alert, he waited. His vision now locked into an arc from where he'd heard the cry. Imagining the reason. Stinger? No, the beach was protected by a stinger net this time of year so it'd be tough luck if they'd been hit.

And then he saw it.

A hand.

His rare moment of quietude at a fast and furious end, Jonah was flat on his belly, arms heaving the ocean out of his way before he took his next breath.

With each swell he glanced up the beach to see if anyone else was about. But the yellow and red flags marking out the patch of beach patrolled by lifesavers were farther away, this part cleared of life bar a furry blot of brown and white dog patiently awaiting his return.

Jonah kept his eyes on the spot, recalculating distance and tidal currents with every stroke. He'd practically been born on the water, reading her as natural to him as breathing. But the ocean was as cruel as she was restorative, and if she decided not to give up, there wasn't much even the most sea-savvy person could do. He knew.

As for the owner of the hand? *Tourist.* Not a single doubt in his mind.

The adrenalin thundering through him spiked when sunlight glinted off skin close enough to grab. Within seconds he was dragging a woman from the water.

Her hair was so long it trailed behind her like a curtain

of silk, so pale it blended with the sandy backdrop behind. Her skin so fair he found himself squinting at the sun reflecting off her long limbs. And she was lathered in so much damn sunscreen she was as slippery as a fish and he could barely get a grip.

And that was before she began to fight back. "No!" she spluttered.

"Hell, woman," Jonah gritted out. "I'm trying to rescue you, which will not be possible unless you stop struggling."

The woman stopped wriggling long enough to shoot him a flat stare. "I'm an excellent swimmer," she croaked. "I swam conference for Bryn Mawr."

Not just a tourist, Jonah thought, her cultured American accent clipping him about the ears. *From the whole other side of the world.*

"Could have fooled me," he muttered. "Unless that's what passes for the Australian Crawl stateside these days."

The stare became a glare. And her eyes... A wicked green, they were, only one was marred with a whopping great splotch of brown.

And while *he* stared at the anomaly, her hand slipped. Lucky she had the smarts to grab the pointy end of his board, leaving him to clench his thighs for all he was worth.

"Honey," he growled, by then near the end of his limited patience, "I understand that you're embarrassed. But would you rather be humbled or dead?"

Her strange eyes flinted at the *Honey*, not that he gave a damn. All he cared was that she gave a short nod. The sooner he dumped her back on the sand and got on with his day, the better. And if a dose of reality was necessary to get it done, then so be it.

"Good. Now, hoick yourself up on three." When her teeth clamped down on her bottom lip to suppress a grimace, and her fair skin came over paler again, he knew there'd be no hoicking. "Cramp?"

Her next grimace was as good as a yes.

Damn. No more finessing. In for a penny, Jonah locked his legs around the board, hooked his elbows under her arms, and heaved.

She landed awkwardly in a mass of gangly limbs and sea water. Only Jonah's experience and strength kept them from ending up ass up, lungs full of sea water, as he slid her onto his lap, throwing her arms around his neck where she gripped like a limpet. He grabbed her by the waist and held her still as the waves they'd created settled to a gentle rock.

Jonah wondered at what point she would become aware that she was straddling him, groin to groin, skin sliding against him all slippery and salty. Because after a few long moments it was just about all he could think about. Especially when with another grimace she hooked an arm over his shoulder, the other cradling the back of his head, and stretched her leg sideways, flexing her foot, easing out the cramp, her eyes fluttering closed as her expression eased into bliss.

He ought to have cleared his throat, or shifted her into a less compromising position, but with those odd eyes closed to him he got a proper look. Neat nose, long curling lashes stuck together with sea water, mouth like a kiss waiting to happen. If he had to have his paddle disturbed, might as well be by a nice-looking woman…

Tourist, he reminded himself.

And as much as the tourist dollar was his life's blood, and that of the entire cove, he knew that with all the Hawaiian shirts and Havana shorts they packed, it didn't leave much room for common sense.

And those were just the uncomplicated ones. The ones who were happy to come, and happy to go home. Lanky

Yankee here—a city girl with clear dibs on herself—had *complication* written all over.

"You all right?" Jonah asked.

She nodded. Her eyes flicked open, and switched between his and finally she realised she was curled around him like seaweed.   ·

Light sparked in the green depths, the brown splodge strangely unmoved. Then, with a quick swallow, she slid her gaze down his bare chest to where they were joined at the hip. Lower. She breathed in quick, rolling as if to separate only to send a shard of heat right through him as she hit a sweet spot with impressive precision.

"May I—?" she asked, rolling again as if to disentangle.

Gritting his teeth, Jonah grunted in response. Having a woman be seaweed on him wasn't necessarily a bad thing. But out here? With a tourist on the verge of cramp? Besides which she was a bossy little thing. Skin and bone. Burn to a crisp if he didn't get her indoors. Not his type at all.

"This is nice and all," he said, boredom lacing his voice, "but any chance we could get a move on?"

"*Nice?* You clearly need to get out more."

She had him there.

With that she got to it, lifting a leg, the edge of a foot scraping a line across his bare belly, hooking a hair or two on the way, before her toes hit the board, mere millimetres from doing him serious damage. He shifted an inch into safe territory and breathed out. And finally they were both facing front.

Not better, he realised as The Tourist leant forward to grip the edges of his surfboard, leaving nowhere for him to put his hands without fear of getting slapped.

Especially when, in place of swimmers, the woman was bound in something that looked like a big-girl version of those lacy things his Gran used to insist on placing on every table top—all pale string, and cut-out holes, the stuff lifted and separated every time she moved, every time she breathed.

"Did you lose part of your swimmers?"

With a start she looked down, only to breathe out in relief. "No. I'm decent."

"You sure about that?"

The look she shot him over her shoulder was forbearing, the storm swirling in her odd eyes making itself felt south of the border.

"Then I suggest we get moving."

With one last pitying stare that told him she had decided he was about as high on the evolutionary scale as, say, *kelp*, she turned front.

Jonah gave himself a moment to breathe. He'd been on the receiving end of that look before. Funny that the original looker had been an urbanite too, though not from so far away as this piece of work, making him wonder if it was a class they gave at Posh Girls' Schools—*How to Make a Man Feel Lower Than Dirt*.

Only it hadn't worked on him then, and didn't now. They bred them too tough out here. Just made him want to get this over with as soon as humanly possible.

"Lie down," he growled, then settled himself alongside her.

"No way!" she said, wriggling as he trapped her beneath his weight. The woman might look like skin and bone but under him she felt plenty female. She also had a mean right elbow.

"Settle," Jonah demanded. "Or we'll both go under. And this time you can look after your own damn self."

She flicked him a glance, those eyes thunderous, those lips pursed like a promise. A promise he had no intention of honouring.

"Now," he drawled, "are you going to be a good girl and

let me get you safe back to shore, or are you determined to become a statistic?"

After a moment, her accented voice came to him as a hum he felt right through his chest. "Humility or death?"

He felt the smile yank at the corner of his mouth a second too late to stop it. Hers flashed unexpected, like sunshine on a cloudy day.

"Honey," he drawled, "you're not in Kansas any more."

One eyebrow lifted, and her eyes went to his mouth and stayed a beat before they once again looked him in the eye. "New York, actually. I'm from New York. Where there are simply not enough men with your effortless charm."

Sass. Bedraggled and pale and now shaking a little from shock and she was sassing him. Couldn't help but respect her for that. Which was why the time had come to offload her for good.

Jonah held on tight and kicked, making a beeline for the beach.

He did his best to ignore the warmth of the woman beneath him, her creamy back with its crazy mass of string masquerading as a swimsuit.

As soon as they were near enough, he let his feet drop to the sand and pushed the board into the shallows.

She slid off in a gaggle of limbs. He made to help, but she pulled her arm away. Didn't like help this one. Not *his* at any rate.

Hull stood at their approach, shook the sand from his speckled fur, then sat. Not too close. He was as wary of strangers as Jonah was. Smart animal.

Jonah took note and moved his hand away. "Stick to the resort pool, next time. Full-time lifeguards. Do you need me to walk you back to the Tropicana?" Probably best to check in with Claudia, make sure she knew she had a knucklehead staying at her resort.

"How on earth do you know where I'm staying?" asked said knucklehead.

He flicked a dark glance at the Tropicana Nights logo on the towel she'd wrapped tight about her.

"Right," she said, her cheeks pinkening. "Of course. Sorry. I didn't mean to suggest—"

"Yeah, you did."

A deep breath lifted her chest and her odd eyes with it so that she looked up at him from beneath long lashes clumped together like stars. "You're right, I did." A shrug, unexpectedly self-deprecating. Then, "But I can walk myself. Thanks, though, for the other. I really am a good swimmer, but I… Thanks. I guess."

"You're welcome." Then, "I guess."

That smile flickered for a moment, the one that made the woman's face look all warm and welcoming and new. Then all of a sudden she came over green, her wicked gaze became deeply tangled in his, she said, "Luke?" and passed out.

Jonah caught her: bunched towel, gangly limbs, and all.

He lowered himself—and her with him—to the sand, and felt for a pulse at her neck to find it strong and even. She'd be fine. A mix of heatstroke and too much ocean swallowed. No matter what she said about how good a swimmer she was, she was clearly no gym junkie. Even as dead weight she was light as a feather in his arms. All soft, warm skin too. And that mouth, parted, breathing gently. Beckoning.

He slapped her. On the cheek. Lightly.

Then not so lightly.

But she just lay there, angelic and unconscious. Nicer that way, in fact.

Luke, she'd said. He knew a Luke. Was good mates with one. But they didn't look a thing alike. Jonah's hair was darker, curlier. His eyes were grey, Luke's were…buggered if he knew. And while Luke had split Crescent Cove the first chance he had—coming home only when he had no choice—nothing bar the entire cove sinking into the sea would shift Jonah. Not again.

Literally, it seemed, as he tried to ignore the soft heat of the woman in his arms.

Clearly the universe was trying to tell him something. He'd learned to listen when that happened. *Storm's a coming: head to shore. A woman gets it in her head to leave you: never follow. Dinner at the seafood place manned by the local Dreadlock Army: avoid the oysters.*

What the hell he was meant to learn from sitting on a beach with an unconscious American in his arms, he had no idea.

Avery's head hurt. A big red whumping kind of hurt that meant she didn't want to open her eyes.

"That's the way, kid," a voice rumbled into her subconscious. A deep voice. Rough. Male.

For a second, she just lay there, hopeful that when she opened her eyes it would be to find herself lying on a sun lounge, a big buff cabana boy leaning over her holding a tray with piña coladas and coconut oil, his dark curls a halo in the sun...

"Come on, honey. You can do it."

Honey? Australian accent. It all came back to her.

Jet lag. Scorching heat. A quick dip in the ocean to wake up. Then from nowhere, cramp. Fear gripping her lungs as she struggled to keep her head above water. A hand gripping her wrist: strong, brown, safe. And then eyes, formidable grey eyes. Anything but safe.

Letting out a long slow breath to quell the wooziness rising in her belly, Avery opened her eyes.

"Atta girl," said the voice and this time there was a face to go with it. A deeply masculine face—strong jaw covered in stubble a long way past a shadow, lines fanning from the corners of grey eyes shaded by dark brows and thick lashes, a nose with a kink as if it had met with foul play.

Not a cabana boy, then. Not a boy at all. As his quick-silver eyes roved over her, Avery's stomach experienced a very grown-up quiver. It clearly didn't care that the guy was also frowning at her as if she were something that had washed up from the depths of the sea.

So who was he, then?

Luke? The name rang in her head like an echo, and her heart rate quickened to match. Could *this* be him?

But no. Strong as the urge was to have her teenage crush grow up into *this*, he was too big, too rugged. And she'd had enough updates about Claude's family friend over the years to know Luke had lived in London for a while now. Worked in advertising. If *this* guy worked in an office she'd eat her luggage.

And as for *nice*? The sensations tumbling through her belly felt anything but. They felt ragged, brusque, hot and pulsey. And oddly snarky, which she could only put down to the recent oxygen deficit.

On that note, she thought, trying to lift herself to sitting. But her head swam and her stomach right along with it.

Before she had the chance to alter the situation, the guy barked, "Lie down, will you? Last thing I need is for you to throw up on me as well."

While the idea of lying down a bit longer appealed, that wasn't how she rolled. She'd been looking after her-self, and everyone else in her life, since she was sixteen.

"I think I'm about done here," she said.

"Can I get somebody for you?" he asked. "Someone from the resort? Luke?"

Her eyes shot to his. So he wasn't Luke, but he knew him? How did he know *she* knew him…? Oh, my God. Just before she'd passed out, she'd called Luke's name.

Heat and humiliation wrapped around her, Avery untwisted herself from Not-Luke's arms to land on the towel. She scrambled to her feet, jumbled everything into a big ball and on legs of jelly she backed away.

"I'm fine. I'll be fine." She pushed the straggly lumps of hair from her face. "Thanks again. And sorry for ruining your swim. Surf. Whatever."

The brooding stranger stood—sand pale against the brown of his knees, muscles in his arms bunching as he wrapped a hand around the edge of the surfboard he'd wedged into the sand. "I'm a big boy. I'll live."

Yes, you are, a saucy little voice cooed inside her head. But not particularly *nice*. And that was the thing. She'd had some kind of epiphany before she'd gone for a swim, hadn't she? Something about needing some sweet, simple, wholesome, *niceness* in her life compared with the horror her mother was gleefully planning on the other side of the world.

"Take care, little mermaid," he said, taking a step back, right into a slice of golden sunlight that caught his curls, and cut across his big bronzed bare chest.

"You too!" she sing-songed, her inveterate Pollyannaness having finally fought its way back to the surface. "And it's Avery. Avery Shaw."

"Good to know," he said. Then he smiled. And it was something special—kind of crooked and sexy and fabulous. Though Avery felt a subversive moment of disappointment when it didn't reach his eyes. Those crinkles held such promise.

Then he turned and walked away, his surfboard hooked under one arm, his bare feet slapping on the footpath. And from nowhere a huge dog joined him—shaggy and mottled with deep liquid eyes that glanced back at her a moment before turning back into the sun.

Definitely not Luke. Luke Hargreaves had been taller,

his hair lighter, his eyes a gentle brown. And that long-ago summer before her whole world had fallen apart he'd made her feel safe. To this day Avery could sense the approach of conflict as tingles all over her skin, the way some people felt a storm coming in their bad knees, and Mr Muscles back there made her feel as if she'd come out in hives.

She blinked when she realised she was staring, then, turning away, trudged up the beach towards the road, the resort, a good long sensible lie-down.

"Avery!"

She glanced up and saw a brilliantly familiar blonde waving madly her way from the doorway of the Tropicana: navy skirt, blinding blue and yellow Hawaiian shirt, old-fashioned clipboard an extension of her arm. *Claudia.* Oh, now *there* was a sight for sore eyes, and a bruised ego and—

Avery's feet stopped working, right in the middle of the street. For there, standing behind Claudia and a little to the left, thumb swishing distractedly over a smartphone, was Luke Hargreaves—tall, lean, handsome in a clean-shaven city-boy kind of way, in a suit she could pin as Armani from twenty feet away. If that wasn't enough, compared to the mountain of growly man flesh she'd left back there on the beach, not a *single* skin prickle was felt.

With relief Pollyanna tap danced gleefully inside her head as Avery broke out in a sunny smile.

CHAPTER TWO

A CAR HONKED long and loud and Avery came to. Heat landed in her cheeks as she and her still wobbly legs made their way across the road.

She wished her entrance could have been more elegant, but since in the past half an hour she'd near drowned, passed out, woken up looking into the eyes of a testosterone-fuelled surfer who made her skin itch, she had to settle for still standing.

Avery walked up the grassy bank to the front path of the resort where Claudia near ploughed her down with a mass of hugging arms and kisses and relieved laughter. When Avery was finally able to disentangle herself she pulled back, laughing. Compared with the stylishly subdued Mr Hargreaves, Claudia with her bright blue eyes and wild shirt was like sunshine and fairy floss.

"What happened to you?" asked Claudia. No hellos, no *how was your flight*. The best kind of friendship, it always picked up just where it left off.

"Just been out for a refreshing ocean dip!"

Avery shot a telling glance at Luke. Claudia crossed her arms and steadfastly ignored the man at her back. Avery raised an eyebrow. Claudia curled her lip.

They might have lived on different continents their whole lives but with Skype, email, and several overseas trips together, their shorthand was well entrenched.

Finally Claudia cocked her head at the man and with a brief flare of her nostrils said, "Luke, you remember Avery Shaw."

Luke looked up at the sound of his name. Avery held her breath. Luke just blinked.

Rolling her eyes, Claudia turned on him. "My *friend* Avery. The Shaws stayed at the resort ten odd years ago."

Still nothing.

"They booked out the Tiki Suite for an entire summer."

"Right," he said, a flare of recognition *finally* dawning in his seriously lovely brown eyes. "The Americans."

Claudia clearly wasn't moved by it. Something he'd said, or the way he said it, had Claudia bristling. And Claudia wasn't a bristler by nature; she was as bubbly as they came.

Avery didn't have a problem with him seeming rather… serious. Serious was better than hives, any day. And like the worrying of a jagged tooth her mind skipped back to the scratch of the other man's leg hairs on her inner thighs. To the hard heat of his hands gripping her waist, calloused fingers spanning her belly, big thumbs digging uncomfortably into her hips. Those cool grey eyes looking right through her, as if if he could he would have wished her well away…

She shook herself back to the much more pleasant present where Claude snuggled up to her with love. Waiting till she had Luke's distracted attention, she brought out the big guns—a smile that had cost her parents as much as a small car. "Nice seeing you again, Luke. Hopefully we'll bump into one another again. Catch up on old times."

He blinked again, as if he thought that was what they'd just done. But it was early days. She had time. To do what, she was as yet undecided, but the seeds were there.

"I'm off duty as of this second, Luke," Claude said, not even deigning to look his way. "We'll talk about that *other stuff* later."

"Soon," he said, an edge to his voice.

Claude waved a dismissive hand over her shoulder, offloaded Avery of half her gear as they headed up the stairs into the resort.

"Are you sure?" Avery said. "You must be so busy right now, and I don't want to get in the way. I can help! Whatever you need. I have skills. And they are at your disposal."

"Relax, *Polly*," Claude said, using the nickname she'd given Avery for when she got herself in a positivity loop. "*You* are never in my way."

"Fine, *Julie*," Avery shot back. Claude's nickname had sprung from an odd fascination with *The Love Boat* that Avery had never understood. Though when Claude instantly perked up as a seniors tour group from the UK emerged from behind a pylon—amazingly remembering everybody by name—it couldn't have been more apt.

Cyrus—who'd been leaning on the desk staring out at nothing—straightened so quickly his pirate hat flopped into his eyes.

Claudia frowned at Cyrus, who moved off at quite a pace. "Welcome to Crescent Cove," she said to Avery, "where heat addles the hormones."

"Is that in the town charter?" Avery asked, grinning. "Did I read it on the sign driving in?"

"Unfortunately not. Do you think it would work? As a marketing ploy?" Claude looked more hopeful than the idea merited.

Avery, whose business was public relations and thus who was paid to create goodwill, gave Claude's arm a squeeze. "It couldn't hurt."

They reached the Tiki Suite and Claudia dumped Avery's stuff on a white cane chair in the corner, oblivious to the bucketload of sand raining onto the floor. "Now, refreshing dip, my sweet patooty. What happened to you out there?"

"You should see the other guy," Avery muttered before landing face down on the bed.

Claudia landed next to her face up. Then after a beat she turned on her side, head resting in her upturned palm as she loomed over Avery, eyebrows doing a merry dance. "What other guy?"

Avery scrunched up her face. Then rolled onto her back and stared up at the ceiling. "My leg cramped, and a guy on a surfboard dragged me out of the ocean. I'd have been fine, though. I am a very good swimmer."

Claudia landed on her back and laughed herself silly. "I've been locked inside with Luke all morning, forced to listen to him yabber on about figures and columns and hard decisions and I missed it! Who was the *guy*?"

Avery opened her mouth to give his name, then realised he hadn't given it. *Barbarian.* "I have no clue."

Claude flapped a hand in the sky. "I know everybody. What did he look like?"

Avery tried a shrug, but truth was she could probably describe every crinkle around those deep grey eyes. But knowing she would not be allowed to sleep, till Claudia knew all, she said, "Big. Tanned. Dark curly hair. Your basic beefcake nightmare."

Claudia paused for so long Avery glanced her way. Only to wish she hadn't. For the smile in her friend's eyes did not bode well for her hope that this conversation might be at an end.

"Grey surfboard with a big palm tree on it? Magnificent wolf dog at his heels?"

Damn. "That's the one."

Claude's smile stretched into an all-out grin. "You, my sweet, had the pleasure of meeting Jonah North. That's one supreme example of Australian manhood. And he rescued you? Like, actually pulled you out of the ocean? With his bare hands? What was that like?"

Avery slapped her hands over her face to hide the rising pink as her skin kicked into full-on memory mode at the feeling of those bare hands. "It was mortifying. He called me *honey*. Men only do that when they can't be bothered knowing your name."

"Huh. And yet I can't even remember the last time a guy called me honey. Raoul always called me Sugar Puff."

"Raoul?"

"The dance instructor I was seeing. Once upon a million years ago."

"Well, Sugar Puff is sweet. Toothache inducing, maybe, but sweet."

Truth was Avery usually loved an endearment. They always felt like an arrow to the part of her that had switched to maximum voltage the day her parents had told her they were getting divorced. *Like me! Love me! Don't ever leave me!*

Maybe the fact that she'd responded unfavourably to the barbarian meant she'd grown. "Either way, the guy rubbed me the wrong way."

"I know many a woman who'd give their bikini bottoms to have Jonah North rub them any which way."

"Are you one of them?"

Claude blinked, then laughed so hard she fell back on the bed with a thump.

"That's a no?"

Claude just laughed harder.

"What's so funny?" *Honestly.* Because even while it had been mortifying, it had been one of the more blatantly sensual experiences of her recent memory: the twitch of his muscles as she'd slid her foot across his flat belly, the scrape of longing she'd felt when she'd realised he was holding his breath. Talk about addled.

Claudia brought herself back under control, then shrugged. "Aside from the fact that Jonah really learned how to pull off 'curmudgeonly' the past few years? He's a born and bred local, like me. You know what it's like when you know a guy forever?"

"Sure. Pretty much everyone in my social circle will end up with someone they've known forever."

Claudia's eyes widened. "That's…"

"Neat?"

"I was going to say 'demoralising,' but neat works too."

"It's the Park Avenue way. Dynastic. Families know one another. Finances secured. Much like if you and Luke ended up together. It would keep the resort all in the family."

Claudia flinched, and shook her head. "No. Don't even… But that's *my* point. Anyway, I don't want to talk about Luke. I don't like him very much at the moment."

"I have no idea why. He's grown into quite the dish. And he seems perfectly nice." There was that word again. It had sounded quite wonderful before, all poignant and time-gone-by lovely. This time it fell kind of flat. But that was just semantics. She'd find another word.

In the meanwhile Claude shot her a look that said she'd quite like to lock the man up and throw away the key, but not before she'd lathered him in pollen and set a pack of bees on him. She might look like rainbows and sunshine, but there were clever, cunning, dark places inside Claude. Places she tapped into if those she loved were under threat. While Avery had shut her touchy tendencies away in a box with a big fat lock, oh, about ten years ago, in fact.

"Well, then," said Avery, finding her smile, "how do you feel about my getting to know him a little better while I'm here?"

"Jonah? Perfect! He used to be such a cool guy, so chilled. But he's been so damn broody nowadays. Laughs at my jokes only three times out of ten. Go shake him up, for all our sakes."

"Actually…" Avery said, then cleared her throat. "I meant Luke."

Claude's eyes snapped wide, then settled back to near normal. "Hargreaves?"

"*Yes*, Hargreaves."

Claude thought about this a moment. A few moments. Long enough Avery began to wonder if Claude's irritation with the man was the flipside of something quite the other. In which case she'd back-pedal like crazy!

Claude put her mind to rest when she said, "You do realise he has a stick up his backside? Like, permanently?"

"So says you." Avery laughed. "I thought he seemed perfectly—"

"*Nice?* Okay, then. You have my blessing. Shake that tree if it floats your boat. Just don't get hurt. By the stick. Up his—"

"Yes, thank you. I get it."

"In fact have at them both if you so desire. *Neither* Jonah Broody North or Luke Bloody Hargreaves are my type, that's for sure."

Avery swallowed down the tangled flash of heat at thought of one and focused on the soothing warmth that settled in her belly at thought of the other. "So what *is* your type these days, Miss Claudia?"

Claude's hand came to rest on her chest as she stared at the ceiling. "A man who in thirty years still looks at me the way my dad looks at my mum. Who looks at me one day and says, 'You've worked hard enough, hon, let's go buy a campervan and travel the country.' Who looks at me like I'm his moon and stars. Hokey, right?"

Avery stared up at the ceiling too, noticing a watermark, dismissing it. "So hokey. And while you're at it, could you find me one of those too, please?"

"We here at the Tropicana Nights always aim to please. Now," Claude said, pulling herself to sitting and reaching for the phone, "time to tell me why you are really here. Because I know you too well to know an impromptu month off had nothing to do with it."

Then she held up a finger as someone answered on the other end. And while Claudia ordered dinner, a massage, and a jug of something called a Flaming Flamingo, Avery wondered quite where to start.

Claude knew the background.

That after the divorce Avery rarely saw her dad. Mostly at monthly lunches she organised. And thank goodness they honestly both loved baseball, or those meetings would be quiet affairs. Go Yanks!

As for dear old Mom, she'd turned on Avery's father with such constant and unceasing venom when he'd left it had been made pretty clear to Avery that once on her mother's bad side there was no coming back.

In order to retain any semblance of the family she had left, what could Avery do but become the perfect Park Avenue daughter?

Until the moment her mother had announced her grand plans for her Divorced a Decade party. And Avery—being such a great party planner—*of course* was to be in charge of the entire thing! After a decade of smiling and achieving and navigating the balance between her less-than-accommodating parents, Miss Park Avenue Perfect had finally snapped.

"*You* snapped?" Claude asked as Avery hit that point of the story, her voice a reverent hush. "What did Caroline say when you told her *no*?"

Okay, so this was where it kind of got messy. Where Avery's memory of the event was skewed. By how hard she'd worked to retain a relationship with her distant dad. And how readily her mother had expected she'd be delighted to help out.

"I didn't exactly say...that. Not in so many words."

"Avery," Claude growled.

Avery scrunched her eyes shut tight and admitted, "I told her I couldn't help her because I was taking a sabbatical."

"A sabbatical. And she believed you?"

"When she saw the mock-up I quickly slapped together of my flight details she did. Then I just had to go ahead and call you and actually book the flights. And let all my clients know I was on extended leave from work and couldn't take any new jobs. And close up my apartment and turn off my electric and water and have my mail diverted for a couple months. And voilà!"

"Voilà!" Claude repeated. "Good God, hon! One of these days you're going to have to learn to say the word *no*!"

Avery pish-poshed, even though she and Claude had had the same argument a dozen times over the years.

"Starting now," said Claude. "Repeat after me—*No.*"

"No," Avery shot back.

"Good girl. Now practise. Ten times in the morning. Ten times before bed."

Avery nodded, promised and wondered why she hadn't brought up the fact that she hadn't had a problem saying "no" to Jonah North. And that saying "no" to *him* had felt good. Really good. So she had the ability. Buried somewhere deep down inside perhaps, but the instinct was there when she really meant it.

But Claude was right. She should have told her mother "no." Well, considering there were more venomous snakes in the world's top ten here than any other place on earth, if she was ever going to toughen up, this was the place.

The Charter North Reef Cruiser was on its way to Green Island. In the engine room everything looked shipshape, so Jonah headed up the companionway to the top deck.

The crew ought to have been used to him turning up on a skip unannounced; he did it all the time. There was no point having a fleet of boats with his name on them if they weren't up to his standards. Besides, his father had been a boatman before him and he knew an extra pair of hands was always welcome.

But the moment he entered the air-conditioned salon, the staff scattered. He caught the eye of one—a new girl, by the starched collar of her Charter North polo shirt, who wasn't as quick off the mark as the others. With a belated squeak she leapt into action, polishing the silver handrails with the edge of her sand-coloured shorts. Odd. But industrious.

So he walked the aisles. The passenger list was pretty much as per usual—marine biologists researching the reef, Green Island staffers, a group of girls who looked as if they'd closed one of the resort bars the night before, a toddler with a brown paper bag under his chin.

His gaze caught on a crew of skinny brown boys, skateboards tucked on their laps, eyes looking out of the window as if urging the island nearer. Part of the Dreadlock Army who lived in these parts, kids who survived on sea water and fresh air. A lifetime ago he'd been one of them.

Fast forward and this day he'd been awake since five. Gone for a five-kilometre run. Driven the half-hour to Charter North HQ in Port Douglas. Checked emails, read the new safety procedures manual he'd paid a small fortune to set up, negotiated the purchase of a new pleasure cruiser he had his eye on in Florida. No time for sticking a toe in the ocean, much less taking it on.

As the captain began his spiel over the speaker system about the adventures available once they hit the island, Jonah slid his sunglasses in place and headed aft.

A few customers had staked out prime positions in the

open air, laughing as they were hit with ocean spray. He didn't blame them. It was a hell of a day to be outside.

When they said Queensland was beautiful one day and perfect the next, they were talking about Crescent Cove. The Coral Sea was invariably warm, a slight southerly bringing about a gentle swell. The sky was a dome of blinding blue with only a smattering of soft white streaks far away on the horizon. And soon they'd hit the edge of the Great Barrier Reef, one of the natural wonders of the world.

He was a lucky man to have been born here. Luckier still to remain. He breathed deep of the sky and salt and sun. He didn't need surf. All he needed was never to take the place for granted again.

He nodded to the staff keeping watch on deck and made to head back inside when someone caught his eye. Not just any someone, it was his waterlogged mermaid herself.

She lifted a hand to shield her eyes and turned her gaze to Crescent Cove. She had nice hands. Fine. Her nails were the colour of her dress—a long flame-orange thing flapping against her legs—and her hair was twisted up into a complicated series of knots atop her head making her look as if she were about to step out onto the French Riviera not a small island on the edge of the Pacific.

Jonah glanced at his own hands knowing they'd be less than fine. Burly brown with many a war wound, and motor oil under his chipped nails. He rubbed his fingers across his rough chin. How long since he'd shaved? Three days? Four?

He shoved his hands deep into the pockets of his long shorts, his forehead pinching. What did he care about all that?

Unfortunately, in the time he'd spent *caring*, she'd turned to face him, all elegant stance and plaintive eyes.

Caught out, his breath found itself caught somewhere

in the region of his gut.And then her eyes narrowed. As if he'd done anything to her other than save her ass.

Then the boat hit a swell, the bow lifting and crashing to the water with a thud.

Squeals of excitement ricocheted through the cabin. But, facing him, his mermaid had no purchase. She lost balance, knocked a hip against the side of the boat, and began to topple—

From there everything happened in slow motion— Jonah's leap over a bench, his canvas shoes landing on the slippery deck then sliding him towards her. He reached for her hand, grabbed, caught, and dragged her back to safety and into his arms.

Her hands fisted into his shirt, the scrape of nails through cotton hooked his chest hair, pulling a couple right from the roots. At the sharp tug of pain, he sucked in a breath. And her eyes lifted swiftly to his. Those odd mismatched eyes. Seriously stunning in such an otherwise quiet face.

"Seriously?" he growled. "I'm going to start thinking these moments are all for my benefit."

She gave him a shove. Strength in those lean arms. "Seriously?" she shot back. Then heaved up a hunk of her skirt, flapped it at him accusingly and shot him a look that said that if she had the superpower, she'd have set him on fire. "All that I know is that thanks to you, I'm soaked!"

"Stick around here, princess, and chances are you're gonna get wet."

She opened her mouth…but nothing came out. Instead high spots of pink burned into her cheeks creating hollows beneath her elegant cheekbones, pursing those kissable lips, and bringing wild glints to those eyes. Not such a quiet face after all. "Maybe next time you decide to go all He-Man, try not to rip the victim's arm from its socket."

She rubbed her arm as if to prove as much, only bringing his attention to the fact that her skin was covered in goosebumps. With the temp edging into the high thirties, that was some feat. Only one other reason Jonah knew for a woman to go goosey when locked in a man's arms...

Testing his theory, Jonah leaned an inch her way, caught the intake of breath, the widening of her eyes, the fresh pink staining her cheeks. Seemed Miss Yankee Doodle Dandy here wasn't as unaffected by him as she was making out.

She swallowed and shoved, with less oomph this time. "Oh, go peddle your He-Man act to someone else for a change."

"No one else seems to need it." The fact that nobody else had ever brought out the urge he kept to himself.

Yeah, he'd heard the chatter since he'd come home; heard himself called hell-bent, a lone wolf. But the truth was even before that, as a kid with all the freedom in the world, he'd known he could count the people he could truly depend upon on one hand. He was glad of that instinct now. Less chance he'd make the mistake of counting on the wrong someone again.

And yet, with this one, it took someone else to wrench him away.

"Mr North?"

Jonah turned to find one of his staff standing in the doorway, wringing his hands, swallowing hard, as if his head might be bitten off for disturbing the boss.

"Sir," said the kid, "we have a Code Green."

"Right." Awesome. He'd asked the crew before they'd taken off to grab him in the event of any major incidents so that he could watch any of the new policies and procedures in action. Code Green was otherwise known as Puke Patrol.

"I'll be there in a sec."

The kid disappeared so fast into the salon he practically

evaporated. Leaving Jonah to turn back to Avery, whose eyes were locked onto his chest.

"Twenty minutes till touchdown, Avery," he said.

She blinked, looked up, then pinked some more. He'd never much been one for girls who blushed, but it suited her. Took the edge off her sharp tongue. Heaven help the guy who fell for one before he was witness to the other.

"You might want to get out of the sun. Get something to drink. Complimentary sunscreen's inside. Whatever you do, get something between you and the big blue. One of these days I won't be around to save you."

Not intending to stick around to see how that went down, Jonah slipped inside.

It was a little under twenty minutes before Green Island came into view: a sliver of land on the horizon that grew into a small atoll of forest-green with a long crooked jetty poking out into the ocean. The cruiser slipped through the reef to park and the passengers staggered off; some clutching snorkels ready for a close encounter with tropical fish, others planning to head straight to a bar.

Jonah caught a flash of orange out of the corner of his eye and turned to find Avery now with a huge sunhat covering her face. Lifting her long dress, she stepped onto the gangplank, her shoe caught and she tripped. Jonah near pulled a muscle in an effort not to grab her. Chin tilted a mite higher, she walked steadily along the jetty, where all sorts of adventures awaited.

Adventures…and dangers. Things happened to tourists all the time—swimming too far, diving too deep, getting knocked off by ingenious spouses.

"Avery!" he called.

She turned, surprise lighting her features. "Yes, Jonah?"

She knew his name. A thick slide of satisfaction washed through him—then he remembered the Code Green. *Down boy.* "Take care."

She blinked, those odd eyes widening, then softening in a way that made him want to howl at the moon.

Hence the reason he added, "Don't get eaten."

The next look she shot him might as well have said, *Bite me*. But when she realised they had an audience, she found a sweet-as-pie smile, and said, "Oh, *don't* get eaten. Thanks for the advice. I'll keep it in mind."

And he found himself laughing out loud.

With a frown and twitch of her mouth, she disappeared into the crowd.

Leaving Jonah to use the respite to remind himself that despite the lush mouth, and the bewitching eyes and the rich vein of sexual attraction she'd unearthed, he didn't much *like* her.

Because he'd known a woman like her once before.

He hadn't realised *why* Rach had stood out to him like bonfire on a cloudy night from the first moment he'd seen *her* until it was too late. Turned out it was because despite her attestations that a sea change was exactly what she needed she'd never left the city behind enough to really fit in. Too late by the time he'd seen it to stop her leaving. Too late to convince himself not to follow. Until he'd woken up in Sydney, cut off, miserable, realising what he'd given up for her, and that he'd lost her anyway.

Returning to Crescent Cove after that whole disaster had been hard. Returning to find *he* no longer quite fitted in the place he'd been born had been harder still. He'd had to remake his life, and to do that remake himself. As if the cove had needed a sacrifice in order to take him back, in order to make sure he'd never take her for granted again.

So no, for however long Avery Shaw flitted about the periphery of his life she'd mean no more, or less, to him than a pebble in his shoe.

Because this time his eyes were wide-open and staying that way. This time he wouldn't so much as blink.

CHAPTER THREE

JONAH WASN'T LOOKING for Avery, not entirely.

He found her anyway, on the beach. Her big hat, so wet it flopped onto her shoulders. Half in, half out of a wetsuit that flapped dejectedly against her legs as she jumped around slapping at her skin as if fighting off a swarm of bees.

Jonah picked up his pace to a jog.

"Avery," he called when near enough, "what the hell's wrong now?"

She didn't even look up, just kept on wriggling, giving him flashes of bare stomach through a silver one-piece with great swathes of Lycra cut away leaving the edges to caress a hip, to brush the underside of a breast, keeping Jonah locked into a loop of double takes.

"I'm stung!" she cried, jogging him out of his daze. "Something got me. A box jellyfish. Or a blue bottle. Or a stone fish. I read about them on the flight over. One of them got me. I sting. *Everywhere*."

"Bottles don't come this far north, the suit protects from jellies, and the flippers from stone fish."

Avery jumped from flippered foot to flippered foot as if something terrible was about to explode from out of the sand at her feet. "Then what's wrong with me?"

Jonah made a mental note to have a talk with Claudia. She always had some crazy theme going on at her resort, with games and the like—surely she could keep the woman indoors and out of his sight.

But until then he had to make sure she wasn't actually hurt. Meaning he had to run hands down her arms, ignoring as best he could the new tension knotting hard and fast inside him.

He spun her around to check behind, wrapping the fall of hair about his hand to lift it off her neck, doing his all to avoid the mental images *that* brought forth. He swept his gaze over the skin the swimsuit revealed round back. Then grabbed her by the chin and tilted so he could see her face under the ridiculous hat. Her very pink face.

"Hell, woman," he growled, snapping his hand away. "You're sunburnt."

Her mismatched eyes widened. "Don't be ridiculous."

He took off the hat to make sure, and with a squeak her hand swept to her hair. Jonah rolled his eyes and slapped the hat back on her head. "Did you bring anything for sunburn?" *Sunscreen perhaps?*

He glanced at her silver bag to find its contents already upended and covered in a million grains of white sand. Clearly she'd been looking in the hopes of a remedy herself. *A remedy for stone fish,* he reminded himself, biting back a smile.

"Don't you dare laugh at me!"

Only made him smile all the more. "Don't tell me you were All Conference in Sun Protection at Brown Mare too?"

"Bryn Mawr," she bit out. And, whoa, was that a flicker of a smile from her? The one that lit her up brighter than the sun?

Jonah looked away, tilting his chin towards the jetty. "There's aloe vera on the boat. It'll soothe it at the very least. At least until the great peel sets in."

"I don't peel."

"You will peel, princess. Great ugly strips of dead skin sloughing away."

Muttering under her breath, she shoved all her bits and pieces back into her bag—including, he noted, a dog-eared novel, a bottle of fancy sparkling water, and, yep, sunscreen.

He plucked the sunscreen from her fingers and read the label. "American," he muttered under his breath.

"Excuse me!" she shot back, no muttering there.

"Your SPF levels are not the same as ours. With your skin you can't get away with this rubbish."

"What's wrong with my skin?" she asked, arms wide, giving him prime view of her perfectly lovely skin. And neat straight shoulders, lean waist, hips that flared just right. As for her backside, he remembered with great clarity as she bent over on his board...

Jonah closed his eyes a moment and sent out a blanket curse to whatever he'd done to piss off karma enough to send him Avery Shaw.

"I'm well aware I'm not all golden bronzed like the likes of you," she said, "which is why I bought a bottle from home. *Ours* are stronger."

"Wrong way around, sweetheart," Jonah drawled. "Aussies do it better."

She coughed and spluttered. That was better than having her eyes rove over his *golden-bronzed* self while standing there all pink, and pretty, and half-naked.

Then, feeling more than a little sorry for herself, she slowly went back to refilling her bag, now with far less gusto. Her drooping hat dripped ocean water down her pink skin, she had a scratch on her arm that could do with some antiseptic and a couple of toes had clearly come out badly in a fight with some coral before she'd remembered her flippers.

Suddenly she threw the bag on the sand, slammed her

hands onto her hips and looked him right in the eye. "In New York we have cab drivers who don't know the meaning of the words *health code*. Rats the size of opossums. Steam that oozes from the subways that could knock you out with its stench. I live in a place it takes street smarts to survive. But this place? Holy Jeter!"

After a sob, she began to laugh. And laugh and laugh. It hit the edge of hysteria, but thankfully it never slipped quite that far.

Jonah ran a hand up the back of his neck and looked out at the edge of the jetty visible around the corner of the beach where his boat and the bright blue sea awaited. Basic, elemental pleasures. Enduring... Then glanced back at the tourist whose safety had clearly, for whatever reason, been placed in his hands.

Whatever problems he had with her kind, there was no denying the woman was trying. Enough that something slipped inside him, just a fraction, just enough to give her a break.

"Come on, princess," he said, holding out a hand. "Let's get you a drink."

She glanced at his sand-covered hand and her nose crinkled. "I don't need a drink."

Knowing it was only a matter of time before he regretted it, Jonah took a moment to brush the sand from his hand before holding it out again. It looked so dark near her skin. Big and rough near all that softness. "Well, I do," he said, his voice gruff. "And I'm not about to resort to drinking alone."

Avery watched him from beneath her lashes. Then, taking her bag in one hand and the arms of her wetsuit in the other, she flapped her way back up the beach, leaving him to catch up. "So long as drink doesn't mean beer. Because I don't do beer."

Jonah watched her walk away, flinching every third step

in fear of having unearthed some other Great Australian Wildlife intent on taking her down. Shaking his head, he dug his hands into the pockets of his shorts and did what he'd promised himself he'd never do again—follow a city girl anywhere. "Pity, princess, you really are missing out on one of the great experiences of an Australian summer."

She cut him a look—straight, sure, street smart indeed— and said, "I'll live."

And for the first time since he'd met the woman Jonah believed she just might.

When her straw slurped against the bottom of the coconut shell, dragging in the last drops of rum, coconut milk, and something she couldn't put her finger on, Avery pushed the thing away and looked up with a blissful sigh to find that the fabulous outdoor bar that Jonah had escorted her to some time earlier was empty.

Jonah North of Charter North. About halfway through the cocktail she'd put two and two together and figured the boat was his. She was clever that way, she thought, fluffing up her nearly dry hair, the happy waves in her head making it feel nice. She liked feeling nice.

Now what about Jonah? Big, gruff, handsome, bossy Jonah. Oh, yeah, he'd left her a few minutes ago to go and do…something. She looked around, shielding her eyes against the streak of bright orange cloud lighting up the dark blue horizon. Oops. Since when had the sun begun to set?

She found her phone in her bag and checked the time. Holy Jeter, she'd missed the boat! With a groan she let her head fall into her hands.

She knew the guy had only taken her for a drink because he'd got it into his thick He-Man head that she'd perish without supervision, but now the cad had damn well left her on an island in the middle of the Pacific, with night falling, and nowhere—

"Everything okay?" a familiar deep voice asked.

Avery peeled one eye open and looked through the gaps between her fingers to find Jonah standing by the table, his hands in the pockets of his khaki shorts, his white Charter North shirt flapping against the rises and falls of his chest in the evening breeze, the sunlight pouring over his deeply browned skin.

The guy might be wholly annoying in an I Told You So kind of way, but there was no denying he was Gorgeous— capital G intended. What with that handsome brown face all covered in stubble. And those shoulders—so big, so broad. Those tight dark curls that made a girl want to reach out and touch. And the chest she'd had her hands all over when he'd pulled her out of the ocean, all muscle and golden skin and more dark curling hair. In fact there was plenty about him that made a girl want to touch...

But not her, she reminded herself, sinking her hands down onto the chair so that she could sit on them before they did anything stupid.

If anybody was going to get the benefit of her touch on this trip, it would be that unsuspecting cabana boy—and, boy, did that sound seedy all of a sudden. So maybe not. Maybe, ah, Luke! Yes, dashing, debonair, dishy Luke Hargreaves. *There you go, that was way better than* nice—

"You okay there, Avery?"

"Hmm? Sorry? What?"

Jonah's laugh was a deep low *huh-huh-huh* that she felt in the backs of her knees.

"How many of those have you had?" he asked.

"Just one, thank you very much." A big one. "I'm fine."

"You say that a lot. That you're *fine*."

She did? Funny, she could hear it too, like an eerie echo inside her head. *I'm fine! All good! Don't worry about me!*

Now what can I do to make you *feel better? Cheer-cheer, rah-rah-rah!*

"I say it because I am." *Mostly.* "And I am. Fine. Just too much sun. And those cocktails have quite a kick, don't they? And—" she pointed one way, and then turned and pointed the other, not quite sure which direction was which "—I do believe I'm meant to be on a boat heading back to the mainland right about now."

Jonah pulled out a chair and straddled the thing, like he needed extra room between his legs to accommodate...you know. Avery blinked fast at the direction of her thoughts, before lifting her eyes quick smart to his, only to connect with all that quicksilver. Cool and hot all at once. As if he knew exactly where her eyes and thoughts had just been.

She swallowed. Hard. Tasted rum and coconut and... whatever the other thing was. The deadly wicked other thing that seemed to have made her rather tipsy.

"Avery."

"Yes, Jonah."

The quicksilver shifted, glints lighting the depths. "Our boat left about the time you started filling me in on why you came to the cove."

Avery swallowed, wondering just how much rum she'd imbibed. She'd told him? What exactly? How she'd been a big chicken and fled New York so as to avoid her mother's mortifying divorce anniversary party?

"To catch up with Claudia," Jonah reminded her when she'd looked at him blankly for quite some time.

"Right! Of course. For *Claude.* We're friends, you know? Have been a *lo-o-ong* time."

No laugh this time, but a smile. An honest-to-goodness smile that made his eyes glow and his eye crinkles deepen. Sheesh; the man didn't need to have a sexy smile to go along with the sexy laugh and all the other sexy bits. But there it was. Talk about a potent cocktail.

"I've secured a room at a local resort, the Tea Tree—"

"Wow. It was decent of you to buy me a drink—" *a kicker of a cocktail* "—in order to ease the sunburn—" *embarrassment* "—and all, but a room's rather presumptuous, don't you think?"

A few more glints joined the rest and his next smile came with a flash of white teeth. The rare and beautiful sight made her girl parts uncurl like a cat in the sun.

"Avery," he said, and she kind of wished he'd called her princess, or honey, because her name in that drawl from that mouth was as good as ten minutes of concentrated foreplay. "The room is for you. Just you. Alone."

"Oh," she said. Then several moments too late, "Of course. I knew that. I just— How do you even know that I could pay? I might be broke. Or tight with the purse strings. Or—"

"We're more than a tourist town. The cove is a real community. All I had to do was drop Claude's name and it was comped."

"Really?" Oh, how lovely! They loved Claude enough to look after *her*? Oh, she loved this resort already. Belatedly she wondered why they wouldn't simply comp it for *him*. Probably because Jonah North was a big scary bear. Or maybe he wasn't big on favours. *She* certainly owed him a few.

"I also let Claudia know I'd make sure you got home safe and sound tomorrow."

Avery's eyes shot back to his. A drink. A room. A ride. Maybe he wasn't such a jackass after all. Huh. Did that mean she had to try harder to be nice to him now too? Saying "no" had actually been fun, like being outside her own skin rather than curled up tight inside...

He pushed back his chair and held out his hand to her, and not for the first time. And not for the first time, she baulked.

She glanced up into his eyes to find him watching her, impatience edging at the corner of his mouth. Not wanting to start an international incident, she placed her hand in his to find it warm—as she'd expected—and strong—as she'd imagined—and roughly calloused—which sent a sharp shot of awareness right down her arm.

"Sorry," she said in a rush of breath as he tugged her to her feet, "my manners seem to fly right out the window where you're concerned. I can't seem to figure out why."

His pale grey eyes now shadows in the falling light, he said, "Can't you?"

Avery's belly clenched at the intensity of his gaze, and her heart beat so hard she could hear it behind her ears.

Such a simple question, with such a simple answer: she could.

She was obnoxious when he was around because he flummoxed her. He made her feel as if she had to keep her emotional dukes up, permanently, lest he find a way in and knock her out.

And if the past few days far away from the drama of her real life had told her anything, it was that she sorely needed a break. A return to simpler times. Like the summer when the most important thing that had ever happened to her had been a smile from the dreamy brown-eyed boy across the other side of the beach bonfire.

"The thing is," she said, regretting opening her mouth even as the words poured out, "I'm currently…thinking about… seeing someone."

"Someone?" he asked, everything in him suddenly seeming very still.

"Well, a man, to be more specific."

Jonah looked about the bar where an islander was putting chairs onto the tables so he could sweep the floor. He hooked a thumb in the guy's direction.

"No!" said Avery, grabbing his thumb and pulling it

down by his side. It brought her within inches of his chest, so that she could feel the steady rise and fall of his breaths, the heat of his skin, could count his individual eyelashes, all one million of the gorgeous things. She let go. Backed away. Breathed. "Someone *else*. Someone I met here years ago. Someone I'm hoping to...*reconnect* with."

"So then you're *not* here to help out Claudia." His words were tinged with such depths of boredom she wondered how she'd even come to think it was any of his business in the first place.

"Of course I am." Avery lifted her chin. And she was. Or at least she would be. But since their big girlie talk, she hadn't been able to pin her friend down long enough for a coffee, much less a conversation. *Go play tourist!* Claude would say on the fly. *Swim, drink cocktails, take a boat to Green Island.* Look how that turned out.

"You city girls," said Jonah, his voice dropping into a by now familiar growl. "Can't relax. Can't do one thing at a time. Can't settle your damn selves for love or money."

"That's a pretty broad brush."

"Am I wrong?"

Well...no. Back home "busy-busy" or "can't seem to get anything done" was akin to "fine, thanks."

"Yeah," he said, ducking his head as he ran a hand up the back of his neck and through those glorious curls. "That's what I thought. Come on, princess, let's get you checked in."

He jerked his chin in the direction of the exit, and this time he didn't hold out a hand.

Feeling strangely bereft, Avery collected her sandy, sodden gear and followed in her wet clothes and bare feet as at some point she'd lost her shoes. Beneath the shadows of the palm trees that grew everywhere in this part of the world, up the neat paths nearly empty of tourists now most had headed off the island.

And her mind whirled back to how that mortifying conversation had begun.

Can't you? he'd asked, when she'd admitted not knowing why she pushed his buttons. But then why did he insist on pushing hers? Maybe, just maybe, she rubbed him the wrong way too. That very particular kind of wrong way that felt so right.

At that moment Jonah looked back, and she offered up her most innocuous smile.

"All okay?"

"Fine, thanks. You?"

The edge of his mouth twitched, but there was no smile. No evidence he thought she was hot stuff too. He merely lifted a big arm towards a small building with a thatched roof—the Tea Tree Resort and Spa—and they headed inside into blissful air-conditioned luxury.

Once she'd got her key and thanked the guy at Reception profusely for the room, promising him payment, free PR services, a night in a hotel in New York if he was ever in town—all of which he rejected with a grin—she headed in the direction of her bungalow.

The clearing of a male throat brought her up short, and she turned to find Jonah leaning against the wall.

"You're not staying here?" she asked, and the guy's jaw twitched so hard she worried he'd break a tooth. "I mean in another room?"

"I have a place on the island."

"Oh." She waited for more. A description would have been nice. A little shanty hidden from view in the mangroves on the far side of the island? A towel on the sand, nothing between him and the stars? But no, he just stood there, in the only patch of shadow in the entire bright space.

"Think you'll be okay here?" he asked, his voice rough

around the edges, and yet on closer inspection...not so much. Much like the man himself.

"You tell me. You're the one who seems to think I can't walk out the door without facing certain death."

"I'll make you a deal," he said, his expression cool, those eyes of his quiet, giving nothing away. "If you're still alive in the morning, I'll change my tune."

"Till the morning, then," Avery said, taking a step outside the force field the guy wore like a second skin. "Now I'm going to take a long cold shower."

His gaze hardened on hers, and she felt herself come over pink, and fast.

"For the sunburn."

At her flat response, his mouth kicked into a smile, giving her another hint of those neat white teeth. A flash of those eye crinkles. A flood of sensation curled deep into her belly.

"Good night, Jonah."

He breathed in deep, breathed out slow. "Sleep tight," he said, then walked away.

Yeah right, Avery thought, watching the front doorway through which he'd left long after he was gone.

When she got to her room it was to find a fruit basket, a bottle of wine, and a big fat tub of aloe vera with a Post-it note slapped on top that read, "For the American who now knows Aussies do it better."

CHAPTER FOUR

AVERY WOKE TO an insistent buzzing. Groaning, she scrunched one eye open to find herself in a strange room. A strange bed. Peering through narrowed eyes, she saw the pillow beside her was undisturbed. That was something, at least.

She let her senses stretch a mite and slowly the day before came back to her... Green Island. Jonah. Sunburn. Jonah. Cocktail. Jonah. And lusting. Oodles of coconut-scented lusting. *And Jonah.*

And she rolled over to bury her face in a pillow.

When the buzzing started up again, she realised it was the hotel phone. She smacked her hand around the bedside table till she found it. "Hello?" Her voice sounded as if she'd swallowed a bucket of sand.

The laughter that followed needed no introduction.

"Don't. Please. It hurts."

"I don't doubt it," Jonah rumbled, his voice even deeper through the phone. "How long till you can be ready to leave?"

"A week?"

She felt the smile. Felt it slink across her skin and settle in her belly. "Half an hour."

"I'll meet you in Reception in forty-five minutes. And don't forget the sunscreen. Australian. Factor thirty. Buy some from the resort shop."

"Where are we going?"

"Home," he said, then hung up.

Avery heaved herself upright and squinted against the sunshine pouring through the curtain-free windows. The scent of sea air was fresh and sharp, the swoosh of the water nearby like a lullaby. It was a fantasy, with—thanks to rum—glimpses of hell. But it sure wasn't home.

Home was blaring horns and sidewalks teeming with life, not all of it human. City lights so bright you could barely see the stars. It was keeping your handbag close and your frenemies closer. It was freezing in New York right now. And heading into night. The storefronts filled with the first hints at hopeful spring fashion even while the locals scurried by in scarves and boots and coats to keep out the chill.

As soon as she turned on her phone it beeped. Her mother had sent a message at some point, as if she could sense her beloved daughter was about to have less than positive thoughts.

Hello, my darling! I hope you are having a fabulous time. When you get a moment could you please send me Freddy Horgendaas's number as I have had a most brilliant idea. I miss you more than you can know. xXx

Freddy was a *most brilliant* cake-maker, famous for his wildly risqué creations. Avery pressed finger and thumb into her eye sockets, glad anew she wouldn't be there when her mother revealed a cake in the shape of her father's private parts with a whopping great knife stuck right in the centre.

She sent the number with the heading 'Freddy Deets' knowing the lack of a complete sentence would make her mother twitch. It wasn't a *no*. More like passive aggression. But for her it was definitely a move in the right direction.

Forty minutes later—showered and changed into the still-damp bikini she'd found on the bathroom floor—

she made a quick stop to the resort gift shop where she picked up an oversized It's Easy Being Green! T-shirt, a fisherman's hat, and flip-flops to replace the shoes she'd somehow lost along the way, and slathered herself in *Australian* sunscreen and handed her key in to the day staff at Reception.

The girls behind the desk chattered about the shock of Claudia's and Luke's parents suddenly heading off into the middle of nowhere, and asked how Claudia was coping. Avery said her friend was coping just great, all the while thinking *shock* and *coping* were pretty loaded words. Making a deal with herself to pin Claude down asap, Avery still knew the moment Jonah had arrived, for she might as well have turned invisible to the two women behind the desk.

"Hi, Jonah!" the girls sing-songed.

"Morning, ladies," he said from behind her, his deep Australian drawl hooking into that place behind Avery's belly button it always seemed to catch. Then to Avery, "Ready to go?"

And the girls' eyes turned to her in amazement and envy.

Avery shook her head infinitesimally—*I get the lust, believe me, but don't panic, he's not the guy for me.*

Then she turned, all that denial ringing in her head as it got a load of the man who'd arrived to take her away.

It shouldn't have been a surprise that Jonah was *still* unshaven, and yet the sight of all that manly stubble first thing in the morning did the strangest things to her constitution. As did the warm brown of his skin against the navy blue shirt, and the strong calves beneath his long shorts, and the crystal-clear grey eyes.

"Shall we?" he asked.

We shall, she thought.

"Bye, Jonah!" the girls called.

Avery, who was by then five steps ahead of Jonah, rolled her eyes.

When they hit sunlight, she stopped, not knowing which way to go.

"What time's the boat?"

"No boat today. Not for us anyway." And then his hand strayed to her lower back, burning like a brand as he guided her along the path, leaving nothing between his searing touch but the cotton of her T-shirt and her still-damp swimmers.

"This way," he said, guiding her with the slightest pressure as he eased her through a gate marked Private then down a sandy path beneath the shade of a small forest, and back out into the sunshine where a jetty poked out into the blinding blue sea. And perched on a big square at the end—

"A helicopter?" A pretty one too, with the Charter North logo emblazed across the side.

"It was brought here this morning on a charter. They don't need it back till four. Quickest way off the island."

"No, thanks," she said, crossing her arms across her chest, "I'll wait for the boat."

"You sure?" he asked, his eyes dropping to where her crossed arms had created a little faux cleavage. Her next breath in was difficult. "It'll be a good eight hours from now, the sea rocking you back and forth, all that noise from a bunch of very tired kids after a long hot day at the beach—"

Avery held up a hand to shush him as she swallowed down the heave of anticipatory post-cocktail seasickness rising up in her stomach. "Yes, thank you. I get your point. So where's our pilot?"

At the twist of his smile, she knew.

Before she could object, Jonah's hands were at her waist, shoving her forward. Her self-preservation instincts actually propelled her away from his touch and towards the contraption as if it were the lesser danger.

When he hoisted her up, she scrambled into her seat with less grace than she'd have liked. And then suddenly he was there, his silhouette blocking out the sun, the scent of him—soap and sea and so much man—sliding inside her senses, the back of his knuckles scraping the T-shirt across her belly…

Oh, he was plugging her in.

"That feels good," she said. Then, cheeks going from sunburned to scorched in half a second flat, added, "The *belt* feels good. Fine. Nice and tight." *Nice and tight?*

A muscle in Jonah's cheek twitched, then without another word he passed her a set of headphones, slid some over his dark curls, flipped some dials, chatted to a flight-control tower, and soon they were off, with Avery's stomach trailing about ten feet below.

It didn't help that Jonah seemed content to simply fly, sunlight slanting across the strong planes of his face, his big thighs spread out over his seat.

Three minutes into the flight Avery nearly whooped with relief when she found a subject that didn't carry some unintentional double entendre. She waved a hand Jonah's way.

He tapped her headphones. *Right.*

"I hope you found someone to look after your dog," she said, her voice tinny in her ears. "I was thinking about it before I fell asleep last night. I mean, since it was my fault you couldn't go home to him last night."

"Hull'll be fine."

Hull. It suited the huge wolfish beast. Like something a Viking might call his best friend.

Then Jonah added, "But he's not my dog."

"Oh. But I thought… Claude said—"

"He's not my dog."

Okay, then.

An age later Jonah's voice came to her, deep and echoey through the headphones. "Want to know what I was thinking about when I finally fell asleep?"

Yes... But she was meant to be getting better at saying no. And this seemed like a really good chance to practise. "No," she lied, her voice flat even as her heart rate shot through the roof.

He shot her a look. Grey eyes hooded, lazy with heat. And the smile that curved at his mouth was predatory. "I'm going to tell you anyway."

Oh, hell.

"I wondered how long it will be before I have to throw myself between you and a drop bear."

Avery wasn't fast enough to hide the smile that tugged at her mouth. Or slow enough not to notice that his gaze dropped to her mouth and stayed. "I may be a tourist, Jonah, but I'm not an idiot. There's no such thing as a drop bear."

His eyes—thankfully—slid back to hers. "Claudia tipped you off, eh?"

"She is fabulous that way."

At mention of her friend another option occurred to her! Sitting up straighter, she turned in her seat as much as she could, ignoring the zing that travelled up her leg as her knee brushed against his.

"Speaking of Claudia," she said. *Here goes.* "She thinks you're hot."

A rise of an eyebrow showed his surprise. "Really?" And for a moment she thought she had him. Then he had to go and ask, "What do *you* think?"

Her stomach clenched as if taking a direct hit. "That's irrelevant."

"Not to me."

"Why do you even care?"

His next look was flat, intent, no holds barred. "If you don't know that yet, Ms Shaw, then I'm afraid that fancy education of yours was a complete waste."

She tried to blink. To think. To come up with some fabulous retort that would send him yelping back into his man cave. But the pull of those eyes, that face, that voice, basking in the wholly masculine scent of him filling the tiny cabin, she couldn't come up with a pronoun, much less an entire sentence.

And the longer the silence built, the less chance she had of getting herself off the hook.

It took for him to break eye contact—when a gust of wind picked them up and rocked them about—for her to drag her eyes away.

With skill and haste, he slipped them above the air stream and into calmer air space. While her stomach still felt as if it were tripping and falling. All because of a little innocent flirting.

Only it didn't feel innocent. It *felt* like Jonah was staking a claim.

But he scared the bejesus out of her. Not *him* so much; the swiftness of her attraction to him. It was fierce. And kind of wild. And she was the woman who calmed the waters. Not the kind who ever went chasing storms.

Even while she knew she was about to admit she understood exactly what Jonah meant, she said, "I told you— I'm interested in someone else." *Considering becoming interested, anyway.*

Then, as if it just didn't matter, he said, "You didn't answer my question."

"Because it's a ridiculous question!"

"You brought it up."

So she had. How had this suddenly gone so wrong?

Avery risked a glance to find Jonah's eyes back on her mouth. His jaw was tight, his breaths slow and deep. And his deep grey eyes made their way back to hers.

"Good Lord, Jonah, first the girls at the hotel were all swoony over you—"

"You noticed?" The smile was back. And a sheen of perspiration prickled all over her skin.

She held up a hand to block his face from sight. "Then Claude mentions in passing that she thinks you're a 'supreme example of Australian manhood—'"

His laughter at *that* echoed through the tiny space till her toes curled. But still she forged on.

"You really need *me* to be in the line-up too? Are you really that egotistical?"

"No, Avery. I'm really that interested. I want to hear you admit you're as attracted to me as I think you are," he said, and not for a second did he take his eyes from hers.

If she hadn't been strapped up like a Thanksgiving turkey she'd have been on him like cranberry sauce. But she was, and she couldn't. And the conversation had become such a hot mess, Avery wished she could go back in time. Perhaps to the very beginning when all that mattered in life was sleep, food, and a safe place in which to hide from pesky dinosaurs.

"You want to know what I *want*?" she asked, proud of the fact that her voice wasn't quavering all over the place. "What I want is for you to keep your eyes on the sky! No matter what you think of my survival skills, I have no intention of dying today."

She waited, all air stuck in her lungs, for him to say something like *I'd rather keep my eyes on you.* But he merely smiled. As if he knew that she was a big fat liar. Deep down in the dark places inside her that she avoided at all costs. The place where Pollyanna had been born: always positive, not a bother, things would get better, they would! No wonder she worked in PR.

When Jonah's smile only grew, she muttered, "Oh, shut up."

"I didn't say a thing."

"Well, stop *thinking*. It doesn't suit you."

The smile turned into a laugh—*huh-huh-huh.* Then,

easy as you please, he shifted eyes front and left her alone for the rest of the flight.

Disappointment and temptation rode her in equal measure, so much so she clenched her fists and let herself have a good internal scream. Because she didn't need this, feeling all breathless and weightless with all the hot flushes and the like. Avery wasn't looking for sparks. Sparks were incendiary. Their sole purpose was to start fires. And fire burned.

She couldn't have been more relieved when the helicopter finally came to rest on a helipad at the end of a jetty belonging to one of the bigger resorts just north of Crescent Cove.

Even better when she saw Claudia waving as if Avery had been rescued from some deserted island.

And, bless his shiny black shoes, there was Luke, leaning against the Tropicana Nights shuttle bus in the car park at the far end of the jetty. Tall, and handsome, with half an eye on his phone.

Hull was there too. The beast sat apart, upright on a cluster of rocks in the shadow of a tilting palm tree at the end of the jetty. Not Jonah's dog? Maybe somebody should tell the dog that.

Avery managed to get herself unstrapped without help. But getting down was another matter.

Strong hands at her waist, Jonah dropped her to the ground. She didn't dare breathe as all that hard muscle and sun-drenched skin imprinted itself upon her and good. The second her feet hit terra firma, she peeled herself away.

"Here's hoping that's the last time you feel the need to come to my salvation."

Jonah didn't second that thought. In fact, even as he stood there, like some big hot, muscly statue, the look in his eyes told her he wasn't on the same page at all. With a shake of her head, she turned and walked away.

"Avery," he called.

She scrunched her eyes tight a second, held her breath. And when she looked back, she saw he was holding out her missing shoes.

Meaning at some point after he'd dropped her at the Tea Tree he must have gone looking for them. Which was actually...really...nice.

She walked to him, hating every second of it. And when she slid her fingers into the straps, her fingers brushed his. And there was the spark. Hard, fast, debilitating.

Their eyes met. One corner of his sexy mouth lifted. *Deny that*, he said without saying anything at all. And her heart thumped so hard against her ribs she dared not look down in case it was leaving a mark.

"Aaaaaveryyyy!" Claudia's voice carried on the air.

Jonah's eyes followed the sound, and lit up with an easy-going smile, one not fuelled with sex appeal and intent. When his eyes once again found hers, he caught her staring. And the next smile was all sex, all intent, all for her.

"Don't say it," she said, walking backwards, using her dangly sandals as a shield. "Don't even think it. The end."

And then she turned, looped her arm through Claudia's and swung her away from the crazy-making guy at her back.

"You okay?" Claude asked. "You looked all flushed."

"Sunburn," Avery deadpanned. Then bumped shoulders with her friend. "Now did you guys *really* drive out here just to get me?"

"Of course we did. When Jonah rang to say you'd nearly been eaten by a giant squid I had to find out the real story!"

"Funny man," she mumbled, "that friend of yours."

"Seems he's becoming quite the friend of *yours*. I've never been on his chopper before. Not once."

Avery turned back to find Jonah leaning on his helicopter watching her. The big wolf dog now sitting at his heels was watching her too.

"What is with the dog anyway?" she asked, distracting Claudia. "Jonah says it's not his."

"And yet there they are, their own private little wolf pack. It's kind of romantic really, in a tragic, Heathcliffian loner-type way."

"Except instead of cold, wet, English moors he wanders a sunny Aussie beach?"

"Exactly."

"Not quite so tragic, then."

Claude grinned. "If you're going to wander anywhere the rest of your days, might as well be here."

Avery opened her mouth to ask if there'd been a "Catherine" to send him wandering the moors/beach in the first place. Then snapped it shut tight. Jonah North was none of her business. Hopefully she could get through the rest of her holiday without tripping over the guy or she'd go back home even more tightly wound than when she left.

They neared the end of the jetty and Avery looked up and saw Luke watching them from his position at the shuttle bus. She stood straighter, smiled big, and lifted her hand in a cheery wave.

Luke shot her a nod. A smile. Just looking at him she knew he'd know his way around a wine cellar. That he knew a Windsor knot from a Prince Albert. He'd slip into any dinner party with her friends back home as if he were born there. And yet she could still feel Jonah behind her, even at twenty paces away.

"Thanks for the offer of a lift," she said to Claude, backing away, "but I think I'll walk back. Stretch my legs. Lunch later? Just you and me?"

"Lunch would be great."

Avery gave Claude a big hug, then wiggled her fisherman's hat tighter on her head, the strap of her bag digging into the sunburn on her shoulder, and headed off.

* * *

Hull padding along warm and strong beside him, Jonah ambled down the jetty towards Luke.

While he waited for his old mate to finish up his phone call, Jonah's eyes slid to the retreating back of the crazy-making blonde in the oversized green T-shirt that stopped just short of her backside. And he brooded.

With Claude the woman was like some kind of puppy dog, all floppy and happy and bright. Waving to Luke she'd practically preened. While with *him* she was a flinty little thing, all snappy and sharp. It was as if she didn't know who she was. Or that she felt a need to be different things to different people. And *then* there was all that talk of her 'reconnecting' with some other guy... And Jonah was a man who appreciated good faith above all. And yet there was no denying her physical response any time he came near. Or, for that matter, his. It had been a while since he'd felt that kind of spark. Real, instant, fiery. And like a fish-hook in the gut, it wasn't letting go. Every touch, every look, every time he caught her staring at him with those stunning odd eyes it dug deeper.

He should have known better. He *did* know better. Seemed his hormones didn't give a flying hoot. They wanted what they wanted. And they wanted restless little tourist Avery Shaw.

Rach had been a tourist too. Even while she'd *insisted* she wanted to be more. Even when her actions hadn't backed it up, even when she'd never really tried to fit in.

Not that he'd let himself see it. He'd been too caught up in the fantasy of a girl like her seeing something worthy in a drifter like him.

When *she'd* had enough of playing tourist and moved back to Sydney, he'd followed. She'd let him, probably for no stronger reason than that it felt good to be chased. While Jonah had given up everything, leaving his home, his friends, his way of life, selling his father's boat, getting a job on the docks as if water were water. Unable to admit he was wrong…

When he'd had run out of money and finally admitted to himself that it was all a farce, she was happily ensconced in her old life, while his was in tatters.

Lesson learned.

His biggest mistake had been thinking something was more than what it was.

Meaning he had to decide what this was, and soon. A spark. Attraction. A deep burn. Nothing more. So long as he owned it, he could use it. Enjoy it. Till it burned itself out.

Yeeeah, mind made up between one breath and the next. Next time he saw Avery Shaw it was game on.

As for her mysterious 'reconnect'? If it wasn't all some story she'd made up and the guy hadn't manned up by now, fool had missed his chance.

"Jonah, my man," Luke called, jerking Jonah from his reverie.

Jonah moved in and gave his old friend a man hug.

"Funny," said Luke, "riding in the resort van got me to thinking about that summer I used to hitch rides in your Kombi, driving as far as it took to find the best surf of the day."

"Ah, the surf. I remember it well."

"And the girls."

"That too," Jonah added, laughing. They'd spent long summers surfing and laughing and living and loving with no thought of the future. Of how things might ever be different.

Look at them both now. Luke, in his suit and tie, phone glued to his palm, a touch of London in his accent. Jonah the owner of a fleet of boats, a helicopter, more. Successful, single…satisfied.

"Found any wave time since you've been back?" Jonah

asked. If he had it'd be more than Jonah had seen in a long time.

Luke bent down to give Hull a quick scoff about the ears, which Hull took with good grace. "Nah," he said, frowning. "Not likely to either."

Maybe not completely satisfied, then.

"Aww, young Claude have you wrapped around her little finger, does she?"

Luke straightened slowly and slid his hands into his pockets, his gaze skidding to their sunny little friend at the end of the jetty. "Let's just say it's taking longer than I might have hoped for us to...set the tone of our new business relationship."

Jonah laughed. Luke had been one of the big reasons he'd even been able to carve a new life for himself in the cove after Rach. He owed him more than money could repay. But not enough he'd take on Claudia Davis. He patted his friend on the back and said, "Good luck there."

"And good luck there," Luke said, the tone of his voice shifting. Jonah followed the shift in Luke's eyeline to find him watching Avery shuffle off into the distance, her thongs catching at the soft sand, her ridiculously inappropriate city-girl shoes dangling from one hand—the shoes he'd spent an hour the night before combing the moonlit beach to track down.

"Cute," Luke added, both men watching till she disappeared into a copse of palms.

Jonah admitted, "She is that."

"She was here once before, you know," said Luke. "Ten odd years ago. With her family. Odd couple, I remember— father quiet, mother loud, dripping money. And Avery? Skinny little thing. Shy. Overly well-bred. Had a crush on me too, if memory serves. Big eyes following me up and down the beach. If I'd known then she'd turn out like that..."

Jonah missed whatever Luke said next as blood roared between his ears and a grave weight settled in his gut, as if he'd swallowed a load of concrete.

Luke.

Avery planned to 'reconnect' with Luke.

The way she'd bounced on her toes as she'd waved to the guy just now, fixing her hair, smiling from ear to ear, the sunshine smile and all. Hell, she'd called out Luke's name that day on the beach, hadn't she?

The concrete in Jonah's gut now turning his limbs to dead weights, he turned to face his old friend to find Luke's gaze was on the water now, following the line of white foam far out to sea. Avery clearly not on his mind. As the guy hadn't a single clue.

Hull whimpered at his side. Jonah sank a hand into the dog's fur before Hull lifted his big snout and pressed it into Jonah's palm, leaving a trail of slobber Jonah wiped back into his fur.

It had been Luke who'd put up the money to buy back his father's boat when Jonah had come back home to the cove with his tail between his legs, calling it 'back pay of petrol money' from the times he'd hitched rides in that old Kombi. From there Jonah had worked day and night, fixing the thing up, accepting reef charters to earn enough money to buy the next boat, and the next, and the next. Becoming a grown-up, forging a future, one intricately tied to the cove, his home.

He'd paid Luke back within a year. But he *owed* him more than money could ever repay.

Which was precisely why, even while the words tasted like battery acid on the back of his tongue, he said, "You should ask her out."

"Who?" Luke's phone rang, then, frowning, he strolled away, investing everything into the call. Leaving Jonah to throw out his arms in surrender.

Which was when Claudia stormed up. "No getting through to him now." Then, shaking her head, she turned to Jonah with a smile. "Now that you've brought my girl home safe, what's the plan?"

"Work," Jonah said. "Haircut, maybe."

"Don't you dare! Your curls are gorgeous."

Jonah glanced down at the petite bundle of energy at his side. A woman who was as much a part of the landscape as he was. A local. Someone who'd stick around. "Your little friend told me you think I'm hot."

"She did not!"

Jonah smiled back.

Claudia gaped at him a moment before she burst out laughing. "Of course I think you're hot. The entire region of females thinks you're hot. Anyone else simply hasn't met you yet." She squeezed his biceps, gave a little a shiver, and then went back to walking congenially at his side.

And *that* was why he'd never gone there with her. Because while Claudia was cute as a button, and local, and available, there'd never been that spark. That all-out, wham-bam, knock-the-wind-from-your-sails spark that he knew was out there for the having.

He knew because he'd felt it.

Twice.

The first woman who'd made him feel that way had made him believe it was real, until the day she woke up and decided it wasn't.

The other one had convinced herself she wanted to 're-connect' with his best mate.

To think, his week had started with such high hopes.

CHAPTER FIVE

FEELING BETTER ABOUT the world after having just signed a lucrative contract to keep his newest luxury yacht on call for clients of the Hawaiian Punch Hotel, Jonah set off through the outdoor Punch Bowl Bistro, Hull meeting him at the door and padding along beside him.

He'd nearly hit the path between resorts when Hull whimpered, ran around in front of him, and nudged his hand with his nose.

"What's up, boy?" Jonah asked, right at the moment he realised it wasn't a what, it was a *who*.

For there at a table sat Avery Shaw.

It had been days since he'd set eyes on her. After the Luke revelation, he'd figured total avoidance was the safest bet.

Now as he watched her sit at the table doing nothing more seductive than swirl a straw round and round in a pink drink the staunched heat clawed its way through his gut like some creature kept hungry way too long, settling with a discomforting ache in his groin.

Before he even felt his feet move Jonah was threading his way towards her.

Hull got to her first, curling around the base of her table and lying down as if he was expected.

"Hey!" Avery said, her face lighting up with surprised laughter. With sunshine.

Then he saw the moment she knew what Hull's sudden appearance meant. Her head whipped up, her eyes locking onto his, lit by an instant and wild flicker of heat, before she tilted her chin as if to say, *I refuse to admit my cheeks are flushed because of you.*

Yeah, honey, he thought, *right back at ya.*

Then her eyes slid past him, to the empty doorway leading inside the hotel. And all sunshine fled to leave way for sad Bambi. What scrape had she gotten herself into now?

His vision expanded to notice her knife and fork were untouched. The bread basket mere crumbs.

And he knew.

Luke. She'd made plans to have lunch with Luke. And for whatever reason, the goose had clearly failed to show.

That was the moment Jonah should have walked away. Considering how much he owed Luke, how long a friendship they'd enjoyed, and the fact that being anywhere near Avery made him feel like a rubber band stretched at its limit, it was the only honourable option.

And yet he dragged out a chair and—blocking Ms Shaw's view of the front door—sat down.

Luke not carving out time for a surf during his first time in the cove for years was one thing. But not knowing when a gorgeous woman wanted to get to know him better? Unforgivable.

And she was gorgeous. Her pale hair clipped neatly away from her face in some kind of fancy braid, eyes soft and sooty, lips slicked glossy pink, ropes of tiny beads draping over a black-and-white dress that made her look like a million bucks. If he ever needed a reminder she was not from here, that whatever spark was between them had *no* future...

Then she had to go and say, "Oh, you're *staying*?"

And that was it. He was hunkered in. His voice was

one notch above a growl as he said, "Nice to see you too, Miss Shaw."

She pointed over his shoulder. "I'm actually—"

"Thrilled to see me?"

She swallowed, clearly undecided as to whether to admit why she was there alone. In the end she kept her mouth shut.

"Saw you sitting here all alone and figured it was the gentlemanly thing to rescue you from your lonesomeness," he said, casually perusing the menu he already knew by heart. He put the menu down, and settled back in his chair, sliding a leg under the table, navigating Hull's big body. Only to find himself knocking shoes with Avery. Her high-heel-clad foot slipped away.

"Really?"

"Hand to heart," he said, action matching words.

Her eyes flickered to his hand, across his chest, over his shoulders, to his hair, pausing longest of all on his mouth, before skimming back to his eyes. And while he knew it was not smart, was *traitorous* even, he enjoyed every second of it.

"Is your dog even allowed in here?" she said, pointing under the table.

He lifted a shoulder, let it fall. "Not my dog."

She leaned forward a little then. Her mouth kicked into a half-smile.

"Well, whoever's dog he is," that mouth said, "he's sitting on my foot. And my toes are now officially numb. He's enormous."

"Huge," said Jonah, lifting his eyes to hers to find them darkened, determined, as if making some kind of connection between man and beast. Enough that he had to fight the urge to adjust himself.

Wrapping her lips around her straw in a way that was

entirely unfair, she asked, "So how did you and Hull meet?"

"Found him on the beach when he was a pup—a tiny, scrawny, shivery ball of mangy, matted fluff, near dead with exhaustion and hunger. Odds on he wasn't the only one in the litter dumped. Probably tied up in a sack full of rocks and thrown overboard. He's been crazy afraid of water ever since. Took him home, cleaned him up, fed him, and that was it."

"You saved his life and that doesn't make him your responsibility?"

"Never bought him, never sought him. Don't get me wrong, he's a great dog. And if he thinks you're a threat to me, he'd like nothing better than to tear you limb from limb."

"Me?" she said, flicking a quick glance at the now-snoring lump under the table. "A threat?"

Jonah shot her a flat look. She was the biggest threat he'd met in a long time.

By the rise and fall of her chest she got his meaning loud and clear.

Then, frowning, she slipped her fingers down the length of beads and stared at the little bits of pineapple bobbing on top of her drink. Most likely because of the elephant in the room. Or *not* in the room as he hadn't showed up.

Rubbing a hand up the back of his neck, Jonah wished he'd simply called Luke and asked where the hell he was. Or at the very least what his intentions towards her were, if any. Hell, he'd done such a fine job avoiding the woman, for all Jonah knew she and Luke could have been dating for days.

That thought clouded his vision something mad, but didn't put a dent in the attraction that rode over him like a rogue wave. The only right thing to do was leave. Walk away. Avoid more. At least until he knew where they all stood.

He quietly schooled his features, looked casually over the restaurant, towards the still-empty doorway. And set his feet to the floor as he made to leave her be.

When the waiter came shuffling up. "Oh, good, your company's finally arrived. Are you ready to order now?"

Jonah glanced back at Avery to find her blushing madly now, nose buried in the menu.

"Um…he's… I guess. Just… Can I have a second, please? Sorry!"

When she looked up at the waiter she shot him her sunshine smile, catching Jonah in its wake. The effect was like a smack to the back of the head, rattling his thoughts till he could no longer quite put them back in order.

"This is my first time here," she said. "What would you recommend?"

Jonah jabbed a finger at the rump steak. "Rare." Motioned to his friend under the table and said, "Two."

"Make it three," said Avery, picking out a pricey glass of red wine to go along with it.

When the waiter wandered off, she lowered the menu slowly, frowned at it a second, before taking a breath and looking up at him. Clearly bemused as to how they'd got there. Just the two of them. Having lunch.

He wished he knew himself.

Avery shuffled on her chair and said, "So, Jonah, did you always want to work with boats growing up?"

"Boats? We're really heading down that path?"

"Boats. The weather. You pick!" She threw her arms out in frustration. "Or you can just sit there all silent and broody for all I care. I was perfectly happy to have lunch on my own before you came along."

"Were you, now?"

She glared at him then, the truth hovering between them.

She grabbed her pink drink and slugged the thing down till it was empty. The fact that she thought she needed booze to get through lunch with him was actually kind of comforting. Then she licked her lips in search of stray pink drink. And Jonah had never felt less comfortable in his life.

He rubbed a hand over his jaw, hoping the prickle of stubble might wake him the hell up, but instead finding his cheeks covered in overly long scruff. The lack of a close shave was just about the only throwback to his old life. When the idea of lunch with a pretty girl was as normal to him as a day spent in the sea, not something fraught with malignant intentions and mortal peril.

He dropped his calloused fingers to his lap, so like his father's fingers.

She wanted to talk boats? What the hell. "My father worked on boats."

"Oh, a family tradition."

Jonah coughed out a laugh. His father wouldn't have thought so. As brutally proud as Jonah was of everything Charter North had become, he knew his father wouldn't have understood. The types of boats, or the number. Karl North had only ever owned the one boat, the *Mary-Jane*, named after Jonah's mother. And in the end she'd killed him.

"He was a lobster man," Jonah went on. "A diver. Over the reefs. Live collection, by hand." No big hauls, just long hours, negligible conversation, even less outward displays of affection, not much energy left for anything not on the boat.

Avery picked up on the *"Was?"*

"He died at sea when I was seventeen. He'd taught me a thing or two about boats before then, though. I could pull a boat engine apart and put it back together by the time I was fourteen."

"You think that's impressive? At fourteen I could speak French and create a five-course menu for twenty people."

"You cook?"

"I created the *menu*. Cook cooked it."

"Of course."

She grinned. *Sunshine.* And when she slid her fingers over the rope of beads, this time he felt the slide of those fingers somewhere quite else. "And your mother?"

"She left when I was eleven. I haven't seen her since. Hard being married to a man whose first love is big and blue. When the summer storms threaten to turn every boat inside out and upside down. When quotas laws changed, or the crops just weren't there. He went back out there the next day and tried again, because that's what men did."

And there you have it, folks, he thought, dragging in a breath. Most he'd said about his own folks…probably ever. Locals understood. Rach hadn't ever asked. While Avery dug it out of him with no more than a look.

Jonah shifted on his chair.

"My turn?" she said.

"Why the hell not?"

Grinning, this time less sunshine, more sass, she leaned down to wrap her lips around the edge of her glass, found it empty, left a perfect pink kiss in their place.

"My parents are both still around. Dad's an investment banker, busy man, Yankees fan—" A quick fist-pump. "Go Yanks! My mother earned her living the Park Avenue way—divorce—and is a fan of spending Dad's money. While I am the good daughter: cheerful, encouraging, conciliatory."

Jonah struggled to imagine this caustic creature being *conciliatory*. Until he remembered her snuggling up to Claude, bouncing on her heels as she waved to Luke. *Luke.* He frowned. Forgot what he was thinking about, or more likely shoved it way down deep inside.

"Even my apartment is equidistant from both of theirs," she went on.

"You're Switzerland?"

She laughed.

Chin resting on her upturned palm, she said, "Between you and me and this dog who's not yours, being Switzerland is exhausting. I didn't realise how much Switzerland needed a break till I came here. You know what my mother is doing right this second? Organising a *party* to celebrate the tenth anniversary of the divorce. Manhattan rooftop, over a hundred guests, yesterday she called to tell me about the comedian she's hired to roast my father, who won't even be there."

The waiter came back with her wine, which she wrapped her hands around as if it were a life ring. "Worst part? She actually thought I'd be dying to help. As if my relationship with my father—such as it is—means nothing."

Her eyes flickered, a pair of small lines creasing the skin above her nose. And when she shook her head, it was as if a flinty shell had crumbled to reveal a whole different Avery underneath. A woman trying to do the right thing in her small way against near impossible odds.

He got that.

With a shrug and an embarrassed twist of her sweet lips Avery gave him a look.

He opened his mouth to say…something, when Hull sat up with a muffled woof, saving him from saying anything at all. Seconds later the waiter arrived in a flurry. Hull's raw steak had been pounded into mush by the chef. Avery's and Jonah's sat in sweet and juicy seas of mushroom pepper sauce.

After the waiter left, Jonah said, "You know what Switzerland should do next?"

"What's that?" she asked, her hand flinching a little as she put her napkin on her lap.

"Eat," he said, shoving a chunk of steak in his mouth.

Her smile was new—soft, swift, and lovely. And Jonah breathed through the realisation that there couldn't *possibly* be any more last-minute saves.

The next time he nearly did something with this woman it would be all on him.

"So what's the plan for the afternoon?" Jonah asked later as they ambled onto the palm-tree-lined path that curled between the resorts and led back to the main street.

"Tropicana, I guess. Track down Claude. Sit on her so that we can get more than two minutes together in a row."

"How's she doing?" *Another scintillating question.* And yet he couldn't let her go. Not yet. The rubber-band feeling was back, tugging him away even as it pulled him right on back.

"Great. I think. Truth is, she's been so busy running the resort I've probably spent more time with you this holiday than her."

Her cheeks flushed as she realised what she'd said. And something swelled hot and sudden inside him. She'd spent more time with *him*. Not *Luke*. Meaning nothing had happened between them. Yet.

"Come on," he growled, pressing a hand to her back as he shielded her from a group of oblivious teenagers taking up the whole path as they headed towards the Punch Bowl.

Jonah kept his hand at her back as they continued along the now-secluded path. And she let him.

When they reached a fork in the path—one way headed straight to the beach, the other hooking back to the rear entrance to the Tropicana Nights—she turned towards him, and his hand slid naturally to her waist.

Wrong, he told himself, *on so many levels*. And yet it felt so right. His hand in the dip of her waist. Her scent curling beneath his nose. Her mismatched eyes picking up the earthy colours around her.

Her voice was breathless as she said, "Thanks for lunch. It was nice to have company."

Streaks of sunlight shot through the palm leaves above and shone in her pale hair and the pulse that beat in her throat. Through the thin dress he felt the give of her warm flesh beneath his rough palm. She leaned into his touch without even knowing it.

It finally drove him over the edge.

"Even if it wasn't the company you wanted?"

Her eyes flashed. Her cheeks flushed pink. Before she could move away, his second hand joined his first at her waist. And he pressed an inch closer. Two. Till their hips met. Her breath shot from her lungs in a whoosh and her top teeth came down over her bottom lip.

He lifted a hand to run his thumb over the spot, tugging the pink skin, leaving the pad of his thumb moist. "Luke is a fool," Jonah said, his voice so rough his throat hurt.

Her eyes widened, but she didn't deny it. Then they widened even more as she lifted her hands to press against his chest. "Is *that* why you had lunch with me? He couldn't come and sent you to soften the blow?"

"Hell, no," Jonah barked. "I'm nobody's flunky. And Luke's a stand-up guy. Doesn't mean that sometimes he doesn't know a good thing when it's right under his nose."

What the hell was he doing? Trying to talk her into the guy's arms? No. He was making sure she was sure. Because he was beyond sure that he wanted to kiss her. Taste her. Hell, he wanted to throw her over his shoulder and take her back to his cave and get it on till she cried out *his* name.

"He's your friend," she said, her fingers drifting to lie flat against his chest. Jonah's heart rocked against his ribs.

"Which gives me the right to call him out. And if the guy thought any place was better than being right here, right now, with a woman like you, who feels like you feel, and smells as good as you smell, and is into team sports as much as you—"

She laughed at that one, a dreamy gleam in her darkening eyes.

"He's worse than a fool," Jonah finished. "He's too late."

Avery's hands curled against his chest. He held his breath as he waited for her to take them away. Instead they gripped his polo shirt, her fingernails scraping cotton against skin, sending shards of heat straight to his groin. And he pressed back until she bumped against the white stuccoed wall beneath the palms.

Then, hauling Avery against him, with an expulsion of breath and self-control, Jonah laid his lips on hers.

He'd expected sweetness and experience—a woman couldn't be that gorgeous and not make the most of it.

What he didn't expect was the complete assault on his senses. Or the searing thread of need that wrapped tight about him, following the path of her hands as they slid up into his hair, deepening where her body arched against his, throbbing at every pulse point on his body.

Not a pause, or a breath, her lips simply melted under his, soft and delicious. And he drank her in as if it had been coming for days, eons, forever. He had no idea how long that kiss kept him in its thrall before he eased back, the cling of their lips parting on a sigh.

Slowly the rest of the world came back online until Jonah felt the warmth of the sunlight dappling through the trees, and the sound of the nearby waves lapping gently against the sand, and Avery, soft and trembling in his arms.

Then she looked up at him, shell-shocked. As if she'd never been kissed that way in her life. It was such an ego surge, it took everything in him not to wrap his arms around her, rest his forehead against hers, and just live in the moment. To forget about anything else. Anyone.

Hell, he thought, reality hitting like a Mack truck.

How readily he'd just caved. And kissed her. Avery Shaw. Claude's friend. Luke's...who the hell knew what? And until that point pain in his proverbial ass.

He dug deep to find whatever ruthlessness he'd once upon a time dredged up to take a dilapidated old lobster boat and turn it into an empire, and used it to put enough physical distance between himself and Avery that she wrapped her arms about her as if she was suddenly cold.

Her voice was soft as she said, "That was...unexpected."

Not to him. She'd been dragging him back to his old self—when he'd been wild, unfocused, all that mattered was following the sun—for days. Not that he was about to tell her so.

He looked at her sideways. "What was I supposed to do with you looking up at me like that?"

She blinked. "Like what?"

"Like Bambi when his mother died."

Her eyes opened as wide as they could go. "You kissed me to...*cheer me up*?"

"Did it work?"

Snapping back to factory settings, her hands jerked to her hips and her eyes narrowed to dark slits. "What do you think, smart guy? Do I *appear* cheerful?"

She *appeared* even more kissable now, her hair a little dishevelled, her lips swollen, and all those waves of emotion coursing his way. She also looked confused. And a little hurt.

Not so much it stopped him from saying, "I don't know you well enough to rightly say."

She reared back as if slapped. "Wow," she said. "I knew you were a stubborn son of a bitch, Jonah. But until right now I had no idea you were a coward."

And without once looking back she stormed away.

Rubbing a hand up the back of his head, he dragged his

eyes from her retreating back to find trusty Hull sitting at his feet, looking adoring as ever. No judgment there.

"She's partly right," he said. "I am a son of a bitch."

But he wasn't a coward. Not that he was about to chase her to point that out. In fact, considering that kiss, he considered himself pretty frickin' heroic for walking away. Until that point he'd been thinking all about him; why he should stay the hell away from her. Not once had it occurred to him she ought to stay away from him. Not until he'd felt her trembling in his arms.

While he'd made the decision to remain cemented in Crescent Cove for the rest of his natural life, emotionally he would always be a nomad. It was in his blood. Passed down from his flighty mother. His voyager father. To all intents and purposes he'd been on his own since before he was even a teen. Walked himself to school. Lived off what he could cook. Skating. Surfing. Nothing tying him to anything, or any place, except choice.

When Rach had sashayed into town he'd been twenty-three, living like a big kid in his father's house on the bluff, life insurance on the verge of gone. She'd been this sophisticated outsider, come from Sydney for a week, and he'd done everything in his power to win her over. The life might not have been enough for his mum, but if this woman could stay, to him it was incontrovertible proof that *his* was the best life on earth.

She'd moved in with him after three days, and stayed for near a year.

Inevitably, she'd grown bored.

And when she left he'd been left completely untethered. Banging about inside the old house like a bird with broken wings.

After his disastrous move to Sydney with its noise, and smog, and crush of people—he'd taken control of his life. Delivering on the promise of his father's hard work.

He might not have time to connect with the better parts of his old life—with the sun, and the sea, and the big blue—but he felt otherwise fulfilled. Better, he felt *redeemed.*

And he wasn't willing to risk that feeling for anything or anyone. No matter how kissable.

Avery was in such a red-hot haze she couldn't remember how she made it back to the resort. But soon the white steps were loud beneath her high heels as she made her way into the lobby.

Mere days before she'd been delighting in her ability to say *no* to the guy, as if it were some kind of sign that with a little R and R under her belt she might have the wherewithal to say the same to her folks one of these days. But *no.* One touch, one deep dark look, and she'd practically devoured him.

She lifted fingers to lips that felt bruised and tender, knowing that not being able to say no and wanting to say yes were two wholly different things, but it was hard to think straight while she could still *feel* those big strong arms wrap tight about her, his heart thundering beneath her chest, his mouth on hers.

Suddenly feeling a mite woozy, she slowed, found a column and banged her forehead against the cool faux marble. It felt so good she did it again.

"Avery."

Avery looked up, rubbing at the spot on her head as she turned to find Luke Hargreaves striding towards her in his lovely suit with his lovely face and that lovely way he had about him that didn't make her feel as if she were being whipped about inside a tornado.

Her invitation to lunch *had* been casual. An honest-to-goodness catch-up. Nothing more. As picture-perfect as he appeared she'd struggled to whip up the kind of enthusiasm required to campaign for more. Yet maybe this whole thing had been a sign. That she needed to up her game.

"Luke!" she said, leaning in for an air kiss.

"Don't you look a million bucks." He looked her up and down, making her feel...neat. If Jonah had done the same she'd have felt stripped bare. "Don't tell me today was meant to be our lunch date."

Yeah, buddy, it was. "Not to worry! I bumped into Jonah." *Argh!* "So he sat with me, and we ate. Steak." *Oh, just shut up now.*

"Was it any good?"

"I'm sorry?" she squeaked.

"The steak."

"Oh, the *steak* was excellent. Tender. Tasty." *Please shoot me now.* "If you get the chance to eat there, try it."

Nodding as if he just might, Luke ran a hand through his hair leaving tracks that settled in attractively dishevelled waves. Even that didn't have her hankering to run her fingers in their wake. Yet every time she saw a certain head full of tight dark curls it was a physical struggle not to reach out and touch.

"You know what? What are you doing right now?" he asked.

Trying not to make it obvious that my knees aren't yet fully functional after your friend kissed me senseless. You?

He glanced at his watch, frowned some more. "Miraculously I have nothing on my plate right this second, if you'd like to grab a coffee."

"No," she said, rather more sternly than she'd intended. But Avery was a Shaw. And Shaws didn't know the meaning of giving in. Look at her mother! She softened it with a smile. Then said, "Dinner. Tomorrow night. A proper catch-up." A proper setting to see if something *nice* can be forged.

"Perfect." He smiled. "Catch you then." It was a perfectly lovely smile. Her blood didn't come close to rushing; in fact it didn't give a flying hoot.

Avery made to give him a quick peck on the cheek, but instead found herself patting him chummily on the arm. Then he headed off, always with purpose in his stride that one. Unlike Jonah who, even as he got things done, had this air about him as if he had all the time in the world.

With a sigh Avery didn't much want to pick apart, she looked up and caught the eye of young Isis behind the reception desk. The girl waggled her eyebrows suggestively.

If only, Avery thought. Even Pollyanna gave a little yawn. By the time Avery slipped back to her room she collapsed on her bed and had the first nap she'd had since she was a kid. All it took to finally find the limit to her exhaustion was making a date with one man while the kiss of another still lingered on her lips.

CHAPTER SIX

JONAH SAT AT the small backstreet pub the tourists always seemed to miss—probably because it wasn't suffocated by a surfeit of palm trees and Beach Boys music. Self-flagellation being a skill he'd honed during the long months spent in Sydney, he'd invited Luke to join him.

"Thanks for filling in at lunch with Avery today, mate," Luke said.

And there went Jonah's hopes for a quiet beer.

Frosty bottle an inch from his mouth, Luke added, "I bumped into her in the lobby after I finally extricated myself from one of Claudia's presentations. All cardboard signs and permanent markers. She has a dislike for PowerPoint I'll never understand." His eyes shifted Jonah's way. "So how was lunch?"

"They do a good steak," Jonah rumbled, then chugged a third of his beer in one hit.

"So I heard."

He and Luke might only see one another once every couple of years these days, but they'd been mates long enough for Jonah to know he'd been made. *Dammit.*

He held his ground, counting the bottles of spirits lining the shelves behind the bar. Luke shifted on his chair to face Jonah. Until, thumb swishing over the face of his phone, Luke said, "In fact we have dinner plans for tomorrow night. Avery and I."

Jonah gripped his beer, even as he felt his cheek twitch in a masochistic grin. He tipped his beer in Luke's direction as he caught his old friend's gaze. "You're going, right?"

Luke pushed his phone aside, a huge smile creasing his face. "Any reason I shouldn't?"

"You stood her up once before."

Luke's smile fell. "Hardly. She'd told me she was having lunch at the Punch if I was around."

"Luke. Man. Come on. She thought it was a date."

"I don't think so, mate. You've got your wires crossed somewhere."

When had his old mate morphed from his wingman into this blinkered, workaholic monkey with a phone permanently attached to his palm? In fairness, it was probably about the time his ex-wife took his heart out with a fork.

Luke watched him a few long seconds before slowly leaning back in the leather chair. "Should be a fun night, though. Those legs. That smile. And that accent? It just kills me."

Jonah tried to sit still, remain calm, and yet he could *feel* the steam pouring from his ears. Luke clearly noticed, as suddenly he laughed as if he'd never seen anything so funny.

With a tip of his beer bottle towards Jonah, Luke said, "So, you and Miss Manhattan, eh?"

"There is no me and Miss Manhattan."

Luke grinned like a shark as he parroted back, "Jonah. Man. *Come on.*"

Jonah settled his hands around his beer and stared hard into the bubbles. "I'm right there with you on the legs. And the smile. And the accent." And the eyes. He'd had dreams about those eyes, locked onto his, turning dark with pleasure as she fell apart in his arms. "But she's my worst nightmare."

The raised eyebrow of his old friend told him he didn't believe it for a second. "From what Claude tells me, she's from money. So high maintenance, maybe."

"It's not that. She's…" Stunning, sexy, yet despite the big-city sophistication still somehow compellingly naive. She could swipe his legs out from under him if he wasn't careful. "A pain in the ass."

Luke thought on it a moment. "Then again, aren't they all?"

Jonah tapped the neck of Luke's beer bottle with his own.

"I've been around the block a few times now," Jonah went on. "I've made mistakes. I'd like to think I've learned when to trust my gut about such things."

"Since You Know Who?"

Jonah raised an eyebrow in assent. "And yet, I can't seem to…not."

"Then lucky for you the man she clearly wants is me."

At that, whatever morbid little tunnel Jonah had been staring down blinked out of existence. He leant back in his chair, and smiled at his friend. "Not as much as she thinks she does."

"Now what makes you think my charms aren't all-encompassing?"

"I have it on good knowledge that she's…in flux."

Luke's laughter rang through the bar. He sat forward. All ears. And, thankfully, not a lick of rivalry in his gaze. "I've been out of circulation too long. Since when does 'steak' stand for something else?"

"Calm down. Steak meant steak," Jonah rumbled.

"But *something* happened."

When Jonah didn't answer, Luke slammed the table so hard their beers bounced. "Jonah North, pillar of the Crescent Cove community, made out with *my* dinner date who is also apparently his worst nightmare. Was this before or after she asked me to dinner?"

Jonah's cheek twitched and his head suddenly hurt so much he couldn't see straight. "Hell."

Luke's laughter was so loud it echoed through the small bar till the walls shook. "Man, you have no idea how much I'm enjoying this. The number of times girls came up to me only to ask if the dude with the palm-tree surfboard was single... And then along comes a sophisticated out-of-towner, not instantly bowled over by your—to my mind—*deeply* hidden charms, and—"

Luke's words came to an abrupt halt as the parallel with the last great—not so great—relationship of Jonah's life came to light. Luke slapped Jonah hard on the back. "Walk away. Walk away now and do not look back."

"Sounds fine in theory."

"Yet far better in practice. Trust me," Luke said with the bitter edge of first-hand knowledge.

Jonah nodded. The *other* outsider had shaken up his whole life until it had never been remotely the same again.

But he'd been a different man back then. Barely a man at all. Alone for so long, with nothing tethering him to his life, that he'd mistaken lust for intimacy. Company for partnership. The presence of another body in his house for it finally feeling like a home again.

His foundations were stronger now. He was embedded in his life. There was no way he'd make the same mistake twice. If something happened between Avery and him, he'd be just fine. Which meant the decision was now up to her.

"You haven't heard a word I said, have you?" Luke grumbled.

"About what?"

"Battening down the hatches. And several other good boating analogies."

"What the hell do you know about boats? Or women, for that matter."

Luke stared into the middle distance a moment before grinding out an, "Amen."

Avery stood outside the elegant Botch-A-Me restaurant Luke had picked for their date, and took a moment to check her reflection in the window. Her hair was twisted into a sleek sophisticated up-do. Her platinum-toned bustier was elegant and sexy, her wide-legged black pants floaty and sensual. Her favourite teardrop diamond earrings glinted in the light of the tiki torches lighting the restaurant with a warm golden glow.

The man didn't stand a chance.

Pity then that as her focus shifted as she looked through the window, she imagined for a second she'd seen a head of darkly curled hair.

Seriously? After the way Jonah had acted as if that kiss was some kind of *consolation* prize. Forget *him*. It was why she was here tonight after all. Only her damn heart wouldn't give up on him. Pathetic little thing couldn't think past the kiss at all.

Suddenly the dark curls moved and Luke's face came into view, and Avery's stomach sank. She wasn't imagining things. Jonah was there. With Luke. And they were clearly a couple of drinks down. Avery's stomach trembled even as it fell to her knees.

"Hey, kiddo! Sorry I'm late."

Avery turned to find Claudia beside her, peering through the window, her wispy blonde hair caught back in a pretty silver clip, and—for once out of uniform—looking effortlessly lovely in an aqua maxi-dress that made her blue eyes pop.

"Late for what?"

"Ah, dinner? I begged Luke to use the Grand Cayman

back at the Tropicana—the new chef I just hired is fantasmagorical. But *he* insisted *we* need to check out the competition. Everything okay? You look a little unwell."

"No. Everything's fine," Avery said, while the truth was she now shared Claude's urge to slap Luke across the back of the head. As for Jonah? Knees and soft body parts came to mind. All four of them at the same table was going to be a disaster.

Her usual MO would be to bounce about, create some cheery diversion to keep every faction distracted before it escalated into something she couldn't control. It was what she'd do back home.

Or she could face the music.

Taking a deep breath, Avery slipped a hand into the crook of Claudia's elbow and dragged her inside. Avery motioned to the host so that she could see her dining party and made a beeline for the table near the edge of the room, her heart beating so hard she could hear the swoosh of it behind her ears.

Luke saw her coming first, and gave her an honest-to-goodness smile that started in his mouth before landing in his lovely brown eyes. She might have forgiven him if not for the fact that she knew the moment his companion noticed it too. Jonah's buff brown forearm with white shirtsleeves rolled to his elbows moved to slide across the back of his chair, as his head turned and his eyes found hers.

Nothing like a polite smile there. In fact, Jonah was scowling at her as if the fact that he'd trapped her into a kiss gave him some kind of right to be upset with her for making a date with another man.

Gripping her sparkly purse so he couldn't see her trembling, Avery dragged her eyes from his and found Luke standing. Such a gentleman, unlike certain others who were giving her a once-over that made her feel as if her sophistication had been peeled all the way back to skin.

"Lovely to see you, *Luke*," she said.

"Evening, Avery. Don't you look stunning?"

"Thank you. As do you."

Jonah coughed beside her.

With a smile she leant into Luke for a kiss. With a light hand on her hip, he pressed his lips to her cheek. *Nice lips*, she thought. *Firm.* The hand on her hip brief but sure. And he smelled great. When he pulled away she waited for that lovely feeling of bereftness that came when a lover was no longer close enough to touch.

And realised with a sense of impending doom she'd be waiting forever.

"Good evening, Avery," said a deep voice to her left.

Avery looked into the deep grey eyes of Jonah North. He'd stood. *Belatedly.* And yet she had to knock her knees together to hold back the tide of heat that swept over her at the mere sight of him.

"Jonah," she managed.

All she got for her effort was a flicker of an eyebrow, and a slow smile. She leant in for a perfunctory kiss, trying not to remember with quite so much clarity the other kiss. Failing spectacularly as his hand landed on her hip like a brand. The touch of his stubble against her cheek was a delicious rasp that she felt at the backs of her knees. And when he pulled away she felt not so much bereft as bulldozed.

She blinked. And when a smile finally reached his eyes, making them crinkle, making them gleam, she realised that she probably looked exactly like she felt.

"Claude," said Luke, "looking just as lovely."

Claudia stood behind her chair at that, her lips tightening as if she was waiting for the "but." But when it didn't come she gave Luke a quick nod. His eyes darkened, before, with a tilt of his lips, he returned the nod.

Then, Mr Oblivious proceeded to help *Claudia* into her

chair. Meaning Avery had to put up with Jonah doing the same for her, leaving her feeling every inch of exposed skin in her shimmery strapless top.

Then Luke sat on one side of Avery looking intently at the menu, Jonah sat on the other staring her down, while Claudia's eyes smiled in relief over the top of a cocktail she must have ordered before she'd ever arrived.

Oh, well. She'd admit romantic defeat where it came to the estimable Luke Hargreaves, but that didn't mean she couldn't have a very nice catch-up with the boy she'd once known.

And if that pissed off the man on the other side of the table, well, he could lump it.

An hour later, Avery was so exhausted from being charming she could barely sit up straight. Taking a breather, she let the fifties torch song in the background and the chatter of the three friends float over her.

"You okay, Ave?" Claudia asked, the second Avery closed her eyes.

"Shh," she said, opening one eye, "I love this song."

Claudia listened. Then hummed in agreement. "Don't make 'em like they used to."

When the men had nothing to say to that, Claude jabbed them both in the arm. "Talk about not making 'em like they used to… Come on. One of you please ask the poor woman to dance."

"Claude—" Avery blushed. And blushed some more when Luke pushed his chair back and held out a hand. With a cock of his head towards the dance floor he invited her to join him.

She felt Jonah's eyes on hers, but stopped herself from looking his way. With a smile she put her hand in Luke's and lifted to her feet before following him to the dance floor to find they were the only ones there.

Without preamble he swung her out to the end of one arm before hauling her back. She grabbed him tight, breathless with laughter, her fingers gripping his upper arms. And then with a grace she couldn't have hoped for he calmed them into a perfect sway.

She glanced over his shoulder to find Jonah watching her, his white shirt doing its best to cage all that well-earned muscle, the collar slightly askew as if he'd torn the top button open in a hurry, his eyes dark and shadowed in the low lighting. Her stomach sparked, her skin tightening. When he lifted his drink in salute, she knew she'd been staring.

Luke felt…nice, safe. He smelled…clean. He danced… really well. The tiki torches about the edges of her vision wavered and gleamed, catching on jewellery, on sparkles in women's clothes. It would have been such a nice story to one day tell their grandchildren…if only she didn't find it easier to wax lyrical about her surroundings than the man in her arms.

Luke started, and turned them both to find Jonah behind him, a finger raised to tap Luke's shoulder. Yet the interloper's deep grey eyes were only on Avery's as he said, "May I cut in?"

Eyebrows raised, a not-so-surprised smile on his face, Luke turned back to Avery for an answer. "What do you think?" he asked. "Should I release you into the clutches of this ragamuffin?"

Should he? Avery felt as if her world were tipping on its axis. But when her eyes slid back to Jonah's and she felt her entire body fill to the brim with sparks, she knew with a finality that tightened her stomach into a fist that nice and safe weren't in her near future.

She must have nodded, or maybe she simply drifted into Jonah's arms. Either way, she didn't even feel Luke slip away, just that Jonah was there. She had one hand in his, his other hand burning a palm-print into her lower back—her whole body melted.

On the edge of her consciousness, the song came to an end. But they didn't stop swaying. Her eyes didn't leave Jonah's. And his didn't leave hers.

He pulled her closer still, till—without either of them breaking any indecency laws—every bit of her that could touch every bit of him did. When he lowered his hand so that his little finger dipped below the waistline of her pants, her breath hitched in her throat.

"Avery," he said, his voice rough and low.

"I know," she said, and as his arms folded around her she leant her head on his chest, the deep thundering of his heart more than a match for hers.

Whether it was the cocktails Claude was knocking back or Avery's sudden rose-tinted view of the world, she couldn't say—but the rest of the night Luke and Claude seemed to get along without sniping at one another. Which was *nice*. Or it would have been if Jonah hadn't kept finding ways to touch Avery. The slide of his foot against hers, resting his hand on her knee, drifting a finger over her shoulder. At that point *nice* was no longer in her vocabulary.

When the last dessert plate was cleared, and the bill had been paid, Claude sat back with a hand over her stomach. "Who's going to roll me back to my big beautiful home that I adore so very much?" She glanced at Avery before her gaze slid to Jonah. "Forget that. I'll be just fine on my own."

With a sigh, Luke pushed back his chair before collecting Claude with a hand under her elbow. She whipped her elbow away as if burned. But Luke took her hand and threaded it through his elbow and locked it there tight. "Come on, sunshine. Let's get back to our crumbling white elephant before it falls into the sea."

"She's not crumbling. She has...elegant patina."

Luke shot Avery a smile, Jonah a told-you-so look, then, with Claude babbling about fresh paint and passion, they disappeared through the door.

Jonah stood and held out a hand. This time there was no hesitation as Avery put her hand in his.

Outside the air was still and sweet, the road back from the beach devoid of crowds, the moon raining its brilliant light over the world. And as soon as Avery's eyes met Jonah's they were in one another's arms.

The moment their lips met, she felt parts of herself implode on impact. Heat sluiced through the gaps, her nerves went into total meltdown until she was a trembling mass of need, and want, and unhinged desire.

The sweet clinging kiss of the day before was a mere memory as Jonah plundered her senses with his touch, with the insistent seduction of his lips, the intimate rhapsody of his tongue.

Desperation riding them both, Avery's back slammed against a wall, the rough brick catching on her top, her hair, her skin. But she didn't care. She merely tilted and shifted until the kiss was as deep as it could be.

It wasn't deep enough.

All those clothes in the way. She tugged his shirt from his jeans and tore the thing open, her eyes drinking in the sight of him as her hand slid up his torso, through the tight whorls of hair, palming the scorching-hot skin, loving the harsh suck of his breath and the way the hard ridges of muscle jumped under her touch.

With a growl he lifted her bodily, till she wrapped her legs around him, her head rolling back as his mouth went to her neck, to her shoulder, the sweet spot behind her ear.

When he tugged her top down an inch, his nails scraping her soft skin, his tongue finding the edge of her nipple, she froze, the tiniest thread of sense coming back to her from somewhere deep down inside. It might be near midnight, but they were in a public place, her legs around his waist, one arm cradling his head, the other beneath his shirt and riding the length of his back.

"Jonah," she said, her voice a whisper on the still night air.

She felt him tense, then relax, just a fraction, but enough that he lifted his head to rest it against her collarbone, his deep breaths warming her bone deep.

Avery opened her eyes to the sky.

When Jonah had asked her to dance Luke hadn't been surprised. He'd been waiting for it. Which meant it hadn't been spur of the moment. Hadn't been some kind of He-Has-Girl-So-I-Want-Girl reaction.

This big, beautiful, difficult, taciturn, hard-to-crack man had staked his claim.

And scary as the feelings tumbling about inside of her at that knowledge were, the brilliance of them won out.

"Take me home, Jonah."

He held his breath, his chest pressing hard into hers so that she could feel the steady thump of his big strong heart.

"You sure?"

She slid a hand into the back of his hair, the tight curls ensnaring her fingers.

He growled, and she trapped the sound with her kiss as she strove to make the best mistake of her life.

CHAPTER SEVEN

AVERY'S FIRST GLIMPSE inside Jonah's place—a shack tucked away in the hills behind the cove—held no surprises; the place was a total man cave.

Surfboards and a kayak lined up on hooks in the entrance hall. Battered running shoes lay discarded on a small pile of sand under a top-of-the-range road bike. A slew of mismatched barstools shoved under an island bench in the utilitarian kitchen the only dining option, and along with a big dark sprawling lounge were a recycled timber coffee table covered in boating magazines and mug rings and a projector screen taller than she was.

Avery glanced back towards the front door; but as the last time she'd checked there was still no sign yet of the man himself.

Right in the middle of a pretty full-on make-out session on his porch, Hull had let out a gut-curdling yowl before taking off into the forest. And if Avery's heart hadn't already been racing like the Kentucky Derby from that kiss, the sight of big brawny Jonah staring in distress after his dog—sorry, not *his* dog—had made her heart flip twice and go splat.

She'd given him a shove. "Go."

After a brief thank-you kiss he'd gone, leaping off the porch, grabbing a man-sized torch from his big black muscle car, and run off into the forest like some kind of superhero.

No telling how long he'll be, she thought as she distracted her nerves by scoping out the rest of his home. Down the solitary hall was one seriously cool bathroom with a fantastic sunburst mosaic covering an entire wall and an old brass tub—the kind you sat in with your knees up to your chin. Leaning against the doorjamb of his small office, with its big wooden desk, a wall of shelves filled with books and knick-knacks, another covered in old maps, star charts, pictures of boats, she admitted that, while the house might be a total bachelor pad, with not a feminine touch in sight, it was seriously appealing. Simple and raw, woodsy and warm. Lived in.

It was Jonah.

Pushing herself away from the wall, she walked unthinkingly through the last door to find herself standing in a bedroom.

Jonah's bedroom.

Her next breath in was choppy, her palms growing uncommonly warm as her eyes skittered over the chair in the corner covered in man clothes. The bedside table—singular—had at one time been a beer barrel, and now boasted a lamp with a naked bulb, a book—pages curled, face down—and a handful of loose change. No curtains shielded the windows, which were recycled portholes looking out over what would no doubt be a spectacular Pacific view.

Her heart beat wildly as her eyes finally settled on the biggest thing in the room: Jonah's bed. It was big. *Huge.* And unmade, the white sheets a shambles. It wasn't hard to imagine his long brown limbs twisted up in the bedding.

Never in her wildest dreams would she have imagined that she'd be in such a position with a man like Jonah North. A man who made her twitch. And scramble. And think twice. And want. The *want* she felt around him was crazy, wild, and *corrupting*.

A man who couldn't even commit to a dog…

Insides twisting, Avery knew the smart thing to do would be to walk away, before the want became something else, something more. She could already feel it happening, encroaching. Heartbreak loomed with this one. Way better to find herself that cabana boy and piña colada and spend the rest of the summer in blissed-out inactivity.

Too late, she thought as warmth skittered over her skin. Jonah was back.

She turned to find him standing in the bedroom doorway, his broad shoulders blocking out the light from the hall. He'd ditched his shoes, and his shirt, and his eyes were as dark as coals.

Any doubts she might have harboured about what she was doing there went up in a puff of smoke. "Everything okay?" she asked, her voice so husky it was barely intelligible.

"All sorted."

"No baby birds to check on? Stray cats to nurture? Just saying I could go watch a DVD or something till you're… ready."

Jonah's smile was swift. Sexy as hell. And predatory.

And Avery was done thinking. The sound of a zipper rent the air; and when Avery's bustier sank forward into her arms she let it dangle from two fingers before dropping it to the floor.

Jonah's smile disappeared. And Avery's stomach quivered as his dark gaze raked her from head to toe.

When her hand went to the side zip of her floaty pants, Jonah shook his head. Just once, but it was enough for her fingers to fall away.

All man, this one. Never asked permission—not to rescue her, not to kiss her. The only time he'd asked was when he'd wanted to dance. As if he'd known that her acceptance was as significant as kicking down a brick wall.

When Jonah took a step her way, her breath caught in her throat, and in the low light his mouth hitched into a grin. She scowled back, which only made him laugh; that deep masculine *huh-huh-huh* that near took her knees out from under her. Lucky for her, suddenly he was there, an arm at her back, his nose rubbing gently against hers.

Then with a nudge he tilted her chin and captured her mouth with all the ease and honeyed smoothness of a man who'd done so a million times before.

Sparks flittered prettily at the edges of her vision before morphing into a deep delicious warmth that curled down her back and into her limbs. And without another thought Avery's hungry hands roved over all that smooth bare skin. The man was beyond beautiful. He was pure, raw, masculine heat, as if he'd trapped thirty years' worth of sun beneath his skin, till the heat of it pulsed inside him.

She moved, just a fraction, sliding her belly against the erection burning between them, breathless with expectation that she'd be thrown back onto the bed and ravished senseless. Then whimpered when Jonah pulled back. Not entirely, just enough to add air between them, allow breath to escape. Till she was left hyper-aware of the smallest touch, every erratic change to the beat of her pulse.

Then his lips were on her neck, and gone.

On her collarbone, then gone.

On the edge of her mouth, coaxing, teasing, then *gone*.

All the while his hands didn't stop touching, sliding over her back, his rough, calloused thumbs riding the curve of her waist, slipping under the edge of her bra, heading south...

Just when she thought she might melt into a puddle of tormented lust, Jonah took advantage. Completely. His tongue dipping into her sighing mouth to slide along hers, one warm hand cupping her backside pitching her closer, the other delving deep into her hair, capturing her until she was in his complete thrall.

Then his thumbs dipped into the waistband of her pants, finding a heretofore unknown sweet spot at the edge of her hipbones until she curled away from him, gasping. Leaving him all the room he needed to lick his way down her neck, her collarbone, his teeth grabbing the edge of her bra and tearing it away so that he could take her breast in his mouth.

She slipped a bare foot around his calf, keeping him hooked; she dug her hands into his hair, keeping him there, keeping him from ever leaving—ever—as his tongue and teeth and hot breath drove her wild. Until he pulled the other half of her bra away with his fingers, his rough, warm, sure fingers, and, caressing her as if she were something precious, sent the most intense pleasure looping inside her belly it near lifted her off her feet.

When his mouth once more found hers, he kissed her till she felt on the verge of drowning. And her knees finally gave way from under her and she landed on his bed with a thud and a bounce. She flung an arm over her closed eyes in an effort to find her balance.

When she opened them it was to find Jonah standing at the end of the bed, half-cocked grin on his gorgeous face. All golden-brown rippling abs. And dark whorling chest hair. Ropey muscle across his shoulders, veins slicing down his smooth brown arms. A deep tan line from his diving watch wrapping about his wrist.

"You are something else, Jonah North," she said, shaking her head back and forth.

The grin deepened, and his eyes roved over every inch of her. "When you find a name for it, let me know. As I'm totally in the dark about you, Avery Shaw."

And crazy as it sounded, that felt perfectly all right with her.

She hauled herself up, curled her fingers into his open fly to drag him closer only to discover the tan line at his wrist was matched by another. This one was a perfect horizon that split the dark trail of hair leading into his pants.

She kissed the demarcation, relishing his sharp intake of breath. She kissed a little lower to find his skin there scorching hot. She pulled back and licked her lips as if burnt to find they tasted like sun and salt and sharp sea air. Like him. When she went in for another lick he slid his finger to her chin, lifted it so she'd look him in his smoking-hot eyes, then bent towards her.

It seemed forever before his lips found hers. Enough time for all her compressed want to collide with what felt like years and years of unmet need and rustle up a very real shot of fear. Fear that this was about to be so good she might never recover.

Then he unhooked her bra with a practised flick, and the fear was smothered to death.

"Done that before have we, champ?"

Her hands sank into his springy curls as he smiled against her ear before taking her lobe between his teeth for a nip. "One of my many skills."

"Many?"

He lifted his head, moonlight through the porthole window slanting shadows across his crooked nose, his hooded eyes, his beautiful mouth. "You asking me to list them?"

"You seem more like a doer than a talker to me."

She got a grin, a slash of white teeth in his swarthy face, before he lifted an eyebrow in mercurial promise and set to it.

Avery wrapped herself about him as he kissed his way down her belly, his chest hair skimming her bare breasts, then he rid her of her pants and G-string in one smooth yank, and his mouth was on her inner thigh, his teeth grazing her hip, his tongue dipping into her navel.

"Lie still, woman," he demanded, his deep grey, eloquent eyes boring into hers.

She bit her lip and tried, really she tried. But the deep scraping pleasure was nearly too much to bear. And then she completely lost control—her control anyway; she was clearly helpless under his—as his rough hands skimmed over her sensitised breasts, caressed her flinching waist, dug into that sweet spot at her hips, then easy as you please pressed her thighs as far apart as they would go.

As soon as he broke eye contact her eyes slammed shut, red and black swirls of light and dark beating the backs of her eyelids as his breath fanned over her a split second before his tongue dipped deep inside.

That was where thought was lost to her as her world distorted into beats of purest pleasure. Of breath, touch, taste. The near painful rasp of his stubble on her most sensitive skin, the gentle wash of his warm breath, the glorious graze of his tongue, and her own heat, collapsing in on itself until all sensation balanced on the head of a pin before exploding into shards of light to every corner of her universe.

He gave her a scant few seconds to just enjoy it, to bask in the wonderment of such a bone-melting orgasm; enough time to get naked and sheath himself in protection before he kissed and nipped his way up her belly, her overwhelmed nerves crying out, her tenderised muscles jumping at every touch.

When he positioned himself over her, she had the ambitious thought to flip him over and give him the ride of his life, but he'd rendered her so completely limp all she could do was slink her body against his, to rain a series of soft kisses along the spiky underside of his jaw, and run her hands down his back till she found two handfuls of glorious male backside.

Then, wrapping her legs about him, she nudged her sensitised centre against his remarkable erection, and kissed him long and hard and wet and deep while she took him deep inside.

Her gasp was lost as he kissed her back, taking more, taking everything as he deepened the connection. Deeper, deeper, filling her with sensation so intense, she was absorbed. Lost in him.

When her eyes caught on his, she felt herself swirling, tumbling, drowning. She held him tighter, drew him deeper, his intense gaze her only anchor. As they—

"Oh, God!" she cried as she split apart before she even felt it coming.

When Jonah pushed himself to the hilt, and again, and again, finding sweet spots the likes of which Avery had never known, every ounce of pleasure was wrung from her. Too vast, too much… She found yet another peak as Jonah's muscles hardened beneath her touch, heat reaching a fever pitch as he came with a roar that shook the walls.

"Hell, Avery," he said an eon later, his voice muffled in the mess of sheets at her back.

"You're telling me."

He laughed, the sound still muffled. While she ran a quick finger under one eye before smoothing a hand down his back, biting her lip to stop any more tears from falling. Pure emotion, exhaustion, the last threads of tension that had built over the past few weeks back home finally finding a way out.

With a manly groan, Jonah rolled away, one arm flung above his head, the other lying between them. After a long moment he moved his arm closer, close enough his pinky finger spun sweet lazy circles at her hip.

Breathing deep, Avery took his hand, lifted it, and

kissed the palm till the heat of him sank into her like a brand. And then empty, like a vase just waiting to be filled, and wrapped up in layers of delicious afterglow, she fell deeply asleep.

Jonah woke slowly, dragging himself out of a deep sleep with the feeling that he'd been in the middle of a really good dream. When he shifted to find the sheets at his hips rather resembled a teepee, he knew; whatever he'd dreamt it would have been nothing on the very real delights of one Avery Shaw.

With a groan that told of muscles well used he rolled over, only to find the other side of his bed wasn't only empty, it was cold. Meaning she'd been up for a while.

Jonah yawned, scratched his belly, then lifted onto his elbow and listened for sounds of her. Felt with his sub-consciousness for a sense of her. That particular snapping heat that sizzled about her like an electric current. But there was nothing.

"Avery!" he called, his voice husky, his legs not quite ready for dry land. "Come back to bed, woman!"

When his voice echoed off the walls and he got no response, the warmth in his limbs started to dissipate.

"Avery?"

In the distance he heard a scratching. Hull at the front door. He'd locked the dog inside the night before, after the odd run for the hills that had worried Jonah something fierce. But that scratching was coming from *outside*.

Avery. She'd let him out. When she'd left.

Jonah lowered himself back to the bed, laid a forearm over his eyes, slid another to the aching bulge between his legs and swore.

Of course she was gone. What had he expected—to be woken with coffee and bagels? That all it would take was one night to render his flinty little American all sweetness and light?

No. He hadn't. But he also hadn't expected her to run for the hills.

The myriad reasons why he'd managed to keep his hands off her till now had meant that instead of going at it like rabbits, they'd got to know one another in the past couple of weeks. While he wouldn't say they were *friends*—the word was a little too beige for the kinds of feelings the woman engendered—they knew enough about one another he'd have expected a little respect.

Jonah opened his eyes and stared at the first tinges of gold shifting across the ceiling. It had taken him months to realise Rach hadn't respected him. That while he'd been imagining a future, she'd seen him as free board and great lay. A man suitable for a season, not forever.

One night together and Avery had skulked out at God knew what time without having the grace to say *Thank you and good night.*

"Dammit," he swore, hauling himself upright to run two hands through his hair. And despite himself he couldn't help going to that place inside himself he'd worked his ass off to leave behind. The part of him that would always be small town, a lobsterman's son. That knew no matter how many boats he owned, how many homes, how many helicopters or tourism awards or dollars in the bank, to a city girl like Avery Shaw he'd never be enough.

Rachel. A girl like *Rachel.* He'd lived with *her* for a year. He'd slept with Avery once. There was no comparison. None at all.

Punching out enough oaths to make a boxer blush, Jonah hit the floor, tore the sheets off the bed, threw them down the hall to be washed. He didn't want to hit his bed that night and catch her scent, even if it was all he deserved for letting her in. To his head and his home. Thankfully his heart was tough as an old boot.

Still didn't mean it wasn't a smart idea to scrub her scent from his skin, her image from his head, and her presence from his heretofore perfectly fine life. If he saw Avery Shaw again in the weeks she spent in town it would be too soon.

When the cab dropped Avery at the Tropicana, the sun was barely threatening to spread its first golden streaks across the dawn sky.

She slid her room card into the slot at the front of the resort, opened the door and padded across Reception, which, due to the hour, was even more quiet than usual.

Except that Claudia was behind the reception desk.

Before Avery could think up an alternative escape route, Claudia looked up with a start; slamming shut her laptop, and looking as guilty as Avery felt.

"Hi!" said Claude.

"Morning!" chirped Avery. "What are you doing down here so early?"

"Oh, nothing. Just…bookings. *So-o-o* many bookings."

Claude's hair was a little askew, her eyes a little pink. She had gone hard at the cocktails the night before and yet here she was pre-sunrise, hours before check in, and all decked out in her polyester Tropicana Nights finest.

More importantly, though, she seemed distracted enough not to notice Avery's walk of shame.

"Okay, well, I'll catch you later then—"

"Wait."

Dammit. Avery turned to find Claudia looking anything but distracted, her eyes roving over Avery's shimmery top, her swishy black dress pants, the ankle breakers dangling from her fingers.

"Yo ho ho! Avery Shaw, you hot dog. You got yourself some Jonah!"

"Shh."

"Who's going to hear? The pot plants? Come," said Claude, scooting from behind the desk to drag Avery over to a sumptuous leather couch where sunlight was starting to hit patches of once-plush rug. "So what happened? Why the pre-dawn crawl home? After all that sexy touching and tractor-beams eyes you two had going on last night I'd have thought you'd have set the bed ablaze. Was it terrible? All smoke no fire?"

Avery sniffed out a laugh. Then laughed some more. Then laughed so hard she got a stitch. Clutching at her side, she bent from the waist and let her head fall between her knees. Nose an inch from an old wad of gum stuck on the underside of the couch, she sighed. "It was...spectacular. Claude, I can't even begin to describe the things that man did to me. On a cellular level."

"Ha!" Claude clapped her hands so loud it echoed through the gargantuan space. "Awesome. But if it was so spectacular why aren't you at Jonah's shack doing the wild thing with that man right now?"

Because it was only ever going to be a one-night thing? Because her itch for him had finally been scratched? Because she knew Jonah well enough to know he'd give his right pinky not to have to go through a talky-talky morning after?

Avery heaved herself to sitting and stared into nothingness. "Because I am a common-or-garden-variety coward."

Claudia took Avery's hand between hers, and waited till Avery's eyes were on hers. "You, my friend, are generous and kind. To a *fault*. But even the best of us trip over ourselves once in a while. Find your feet again, and you'll be fine."

Avery plucked a mint leaf—left over from some cocktail or other from the night before—from Claude's hair. She just had to figure out which direction her feet ought to be going.

She wondered if he was awake yet. If he knew she was gone. If the decision as to what her summer entailed was already out of her hands.

"So it's all over for you and Luke," Claude said, "one would think."

Avery laughed, then cringed. "Do you think he had any idea that I had…intentions?" Vague, and reactionary, as they'd been.

Claude's mouth twisted in an effort not to smile. "If it makes you feel any better I had a huge case of the hero-worships for the guy when I was a kid."

"Re-e-eally?"

Claudia slapped her on the arm at her saucy tone. "That was, of course, until I realised he was a robot. Thank goodness for Jonah or you might yet have married Luke and moved to wet old London and made robot babies."

Claudia shivered—but whether it was the thought of London weather or making babies with Luke, Avery couldn't be sure.

"What about you? Seeing anyone? Since Raoul?"

"Too busy," Claude said with a wistful sigh. "No time. No energy. Especially for the likes of Raoul."

"Stuff Raoul. Stuff Luke. You should have a fling with some hot blond surfie type, who has big brown muscles and never wears shoes and says dude a lot."

"Not leaving much room for movement there."

"It's a beach. In Australia. Walk outside right now and you'll trip over half a dozen of them."

Claudia checked her phone as if checking the time to see if she could squeeze in a quick fling, then saw she'd missed a message. And her whole demeanour changed:

back stiffening, her eyebrows flying high. "It's Luke," she said. "He's gone."

"What? Where?"

"London."

"When?"

"Some time between when he dropped me back at the resort last night and now. *Dammit.* We had the best conversation we've had all summer last night. About the old days, the mischief we used to get up to behind the scenes in this place, and the crazy plans we made for when we got to take over the resort, and how we used to watch *The Love Boat....* And *then* he ditches me...*us* faster than a speeding bullet?" Frowning, Claudia pressed a thumb to her temple. "Jerk."

"Why?"

"Why is he a jerk? Let me count the ways—"

"No, why did he leave?"

Claudia waved her phone at Avery, too fast for her to catch a word. "'Important Work.' More important than here? His birthright? This place is the entire reason he's as successful as he is!" Claudia nibbled at a fingernail, her right knee shaking so hard it creaked, and stared over at the desk. "I'd better get back."

Avery's eyes glanced off her friend's less than perfect chignon, the dark smudges under her sunny blue eyes. The curve of her shoulders since Luke's message. It was obvious things weren't as peachy as Claude was making out; even Avery could see the resort wasn't as busy as it ought to have been at the height of summer. But she knew her stubborn little friend well enough to know that Claude would come to her in her own time.

Till then, Avery worked her magic the way she best knew how. She took Claude's stressed little face in her hands, removed a bobby pin, smoothed the errant hair into place, and slid the pin back in. "There, there. All better. Now, my clever, inventive, wonderful friend, go get 'em."

Claude sighed out a smile, and then tottered off, her hips swinging in her shiny navy capris, the yellow and blue Hawaiian-print shirt somehow working for her.

Good deed for the day done, Avery lay back on the couch. Unfortunately the second she closed her eyes the night she'd been holding at bay came swarming back to her.

Jonah's mouth on hers, tasting her as if she were precious, delicious, a delicacy he couldn't get enough of. His calloused touch making paths all over her body.

She snapped her eyes open, early morning light reflecting off the white columns and walls.

At least Luke had had the good grace to let Claudia know when he'd done a runner. Avery had dressed in the dark, called a cab and split. Even if none of her expensive schools had given classes on Mornings After, she was well aware that it was just bad form.

She pulled herself up and padded back to her room. She needed a shower. She needed a coffee. Then, as usual, it was up to her to put the world back to rights.

CHAPTER EIGHT

AVERY REALLY GOT the hang of the right-hand drive in Claudia's car—a bright yellow hatchback named Mabel with Tropicana Nights's logo emblazoned over every possible surface—about the time she hit Port Douglas.

The GPS on her phone led her to Charter North's operations, down a long straight road past a bright green golf course, million-dollar homes, and ten-million-dollar views.

She eased through the high gate and pulled to a halt by a security guard in a booth.

To her left was a car park big enough to fit fifty-odd cars, with a dozen gleaming sky-blue Charter North charter buses lined up beside a neat glass and brick building. Oceanside was a perfect row of crisp white sheds, as big as light airplane hangars, the Charter North logo on each catching glints of sunshine.

She knew the guy owned a few boats. And a helicopter. And a shack. Now nautical empire didn't seem such a stretch.

"Ma'am?" the security guard said, bringing her back to earth.

"Sorry. Ah, Avery Shaw to see Jonah North."

He took down her licence plate and let her through with a smile. She pulled into a car park in time for a super-friendly man in chinos and a navy polo shirt—who introduced himself as Tim the office manager—to point the way to a big white building hovering over the water. To Jonah. She would have known anyway, as right in a patch of sun outside lay Hull.

The sun beat down on her flowy shirt, and her bare legs beneath her short shorts. Her silver sandals slapped against the wood of the jetty and Hull lifted his speckled head at her approach.

"Hey, Hull," she whispered. His tail gave three solid thumps—meaning he at least wasn't about to eat her alive for dissing his master—then he went back to guarding the door. Her heart took up the rhythm; whumping so loud she feared it might echo.

The door was open a crack so she snuck inside—and understood instantly why Hull was stationed outside. Jonah had said the dog hated water, and inside huge jetties criss-crossed the floor and a ways below the ocean bobbed and swished against the pylons holding the building suspended above the waves.

A few boats were hooked to the walls by high-tech electrical arms, one in the process of being fixed. Yet another was getting a wash, and spray flew over the top and onto the jetty.

Not seeing any other movement, Avery eased that way, taking care where she stepped as the wood beneath her feet grew wet.

Until against one wall she saw a familiar surfboard. Silvery-grey, like its owner's eyes, with the shadow of a great palm tree right down the middle, and her heart beat so hard it filled her throat.

Because she knew why she'd fled in the middle of the night. Somehow in the odd sequence of meetings that had led her to Jonah's bed, she'd got to know the guy. And despite his ornery moods she even *liked* him.

She'd woken up terrified that those feelings would unleash her Pollyanna side upon him—*Like me! Love me!*—

like some rabid pixie hell-bent on smothering the world with fairy dust. Not quite so terrified, though, as what it might mean if Pollyanna still didn't show up at all.

Her feet felt numb as she came upon a curled-up hose, water trickling from its mouth. Then around the bow of the boat she found suds. And at the end of a great big sponge was Jonah. Feet bare, sopping wet jean shorts clinging to his strong thighs, T-shirt clinging wet to the dips and planes of his gorgeous chest.

As Avery's gaze swept over him, over his roguish dark hair, over the curve of his backside, his athletic legs, she didn't realise how dry her mouth had become until she opened it to talk. "You could hire people to do that, you know."

Jonah stilled. Then his deep grey eyes lifted and caught on her. She felt the look like a hook through the belly—yet he gave nothing away.

A moment later, he turned off the hose, threw the sponge into a bucket at his feet, wiped his forearm across his forehead, and slowly headed her way.

And when he spoke his deep Australian drawl twisted the hook so deep inside she was sure it would leave a scar. "I have hired people to do this." A beat, then, "But today I find being around water a damn fine release of tension."

Avery considered picking up the sponge herself. "Well, that's why I'm here, actually."

"To wash my boat?" His voice skittered down her arms like his touch—coarse and gentle all at once. How did the guy make even *that* sound sexy?

"To apologise."

"For?"

He was going to make her say it, wasn't he? *Not nice.* Not nasty either, though. Just…plain-spoken. Direct. True.

"For leaving. This morning. After—" She waved a hand to cover the rest.

"After you fell asleep in my bed, exhausted from all the hot lovin'."

"Jonah North," she muttered, throwing her hands in the air in despair, "last of the great romantics."

"It was sex, Avery," he said, walking towards her again. "Good sex. Nothing to apologise for."

He didn't stop till he was close enough she could feel his warmth infusing the air around her. Could see his eyelashes all spiked together with water, as they had been that first day. And that his face was a picture of frayed patience, also as it had been that first day.

But the difference between that day and now was vast.

"It was more than good," she said, her voice as jerky as a rusty chainsaw.

One eyebrow lifted along with the corner of his mouth.

"It was freakin' stupendous."

His mouth tilted fully into a smile so sexy it made her vision blur. Then he ran a hand up the back of his hair and said, "Yeah. I'll give you that."

Then he moved nearer, near enough to touch. But instead of touching her, he reached out for a towel draped over a mossy post near her feet. She closed her eyes and prayed for mercy, lest she drool and lose the high ground completely.

Jonah wiped the towel over his face, and down his arms, smearing the sweat and suds.

"Why, then, did you run?"

"I didn't run. I caught a cab."

By the way his brow collapsed over his eyes, she was pretty sure that being flip wasn't going to cut it. But there was no way on God's green earth she was about to tell him she ran because of *how* much she wanted to stay. She'd been very careful till now not to let anyone have that much sway over her desires. Keeping things light, happy, above the surface. The flipside was unthinkable.

"Just hit me with it, Avery," he said, throwing the towel over the back of his neck and holding onto the ends, his biceps bulging without any effort at all. "It's about Luke."

"What? No! Luke was…a brief flirtation with finding a way to distract myself from the goings-on back home by dipping my toes back into the past. But from pretty much the moment you hauled me out of the ocean and manhandled me back to shore and glared down at me with your steamy eyes…" Okay, heading off track now. She breathed deep, her cheeks beginning to heat with a slow burn that showed no signs of stopping, and said, "I want you."

Jonah didn't so much as twitch. He let her sway in the wind. Getting his money's worth. Till finally he said, "Okay, then."

"Okay, then?" That was it? That was all she got? For basically telling the guy he turned her to putty?

He took a step her way but Avery planted her feet into the floor so as not to sway back. "Was there something else?"

"Yeah. You're an ass, Jonah North. A gorgeous ass, one I can't seem to get out of my head no matter how much I try, but still an ass. I'll see you 'round."

She turned and walked away, waving a hand over her shoulder that might have had a certain finger raised. But she'd given her apology and *that* was all that was important. She had the high road. He only had her pride.

Then suddenly he was walking beside her.

"So," he said, "I was just about to head up to the Cape to check on a tour-boat operation I'm thinking of buying."

"How nice for you."

"Avery," he said, his voice a growl as he slid a hand into her elbow, forcing her to stop and look at him. She crossed her arms and glared, as if facing all that sun-soaked skin, and those deep grey eyes, and that pure masculine beauty were some kind of chore.

He tipped his face to the ceiling and muttered, "God, I'm going to regret this. Would you care to join me?"

Pollyanna showed up long enough to flip over and waggle her happy feet in the air. But Avery's dark side, her careful side, pulled Pollyanna's plaits and told her to shut the hell up for a second.

This wasn't as simple as being forgiven. *This* was the tipping point. Her chance to hole up with her heart and spend her summer reading, and swimming, and refilling her emotional well; or to dive into uncharted waters with no clue as to the dangers that lay beneath.

"Are you asking me on a date, Jonah North?"

He watched her for a few seconds, his eyes sliding to settle on her mouth, then with a hard heavy breath he said, "I'll let you decide when we get there."

Because there was no choice really. She *was* going with him. He knew it, and she knew it too.

Avery leant against the battered Jeep that had brought them to the edge of the crumbling jetty on the side of the marshy river, watching Jonah grumble his way through a business call.

He shot her the occasional apologetic glance, but honestly she could have stayed there all day, watching him pace, listening to that voice; it was nearly enough for her to forgive him the hat—a tatty Red Sox cap that he'd foraged from who knew where, as if the fates one day knew she'd be owed some payback.

Avery turned when she heard a boat. It appeared through the tall reeds; not as fast and streamlined as the boat to Green Island, or sleek and sexy as the one Jonah had been washing down back at Charter North HQ. This was squat, low riding, desperately in need of a paint job.

And had Cape Croc Tours written on the side.

While Jonah chatted with the tour operator, Hull—

who'd been pacing back and forth by the Jeep, one eye on the water the other on the man-who-was-not-his-master—huffed at her with a definite air of *You asked for it.*

Jonah rang off, slid the phone into the back pocket of his shorts, and came to her, long strides eating up the dusty ground. While she subjugated her panic beneath a smile.

"You okay?" he asked, and she dialled the smile back a notch.

"Fine! What girl doesn't dream about the day a guy offers to take her on a croc tour? Okay? No. I'm not okay. Are you freakin' kidding me?"

A grin curved across his mouth. Then he reached into the cabin of the Jeep and pulled out an old felt hat and slapped it on her head. Not the most glamorous thing she'd ever worn.

"Can they climb in the boat?"

"The crocs? No."

Hull huffed as if to say Jonah was pulling her leg. Avery glanced back to find him lying in a patch of shade by the Jeep, his head lying disconsolately on his front paws. In fact, maybe she ought to keep him company—

"Ready?" Jonah asked.

"As I'll ever be."

Avery took Jonah's hand as she stepped into the boat, gripping harder as the boat swayed under her feet. Jonah didn't let go till he sat her on a vinyl padded bench at the rear of the vessel.

Feeling a little less terrified, she caught his eye and smiled. "I like your shirt, by the way."

He glanced down at the faded American flag with the eagle emblazoned across it, pulling it away from his chest for a better look and giving her an eyeful of his gorgeous brown stomach.

"Were you thinking of me when you picked it out this morning?"

His deep eyes slunk back to hers, then in a voice deeper than the water below he said, "Believe it or not, princess, I go entire minutes without thinking of you."

Her smile turned into a grin. "Good for you."

He flipped some keys into the air, and caught them, then moved to sit on what looked like a modified barstool up near the helm.

"You're driving?" she called.

"Yep."

"Shouldn't we have a chaperone?" She earned a lift of two dark eyebrows for her efforts. "I mean because the boat's not yours."

Jonah glanced back at the dock. "If we go down he can have the Jeep. And the dog."

"The dog that's not your dog."

His eyes slid back to hers with a sexy smile.

"Fine. Whatever," she said, tipping her hat lower on her head and squinting against the sun. Just the two of them, heading off into the wilderness, where crocs were near guaranteed. She *really* hoped he'd forgiven her for sneaking out on him.

The engine turned over and the boat shifted in the water, giving her a fair spray of river water in the face. Gripping the bench, she looked back over her shoulder and saw how low the boat actually was. The edges of the thing looked real easy to scale. With an agility she wasn't aware she had she scuttled up to take the stool next to Jonah's.

"Happier there?"

"Better view." Her disobedient gaze landed on his muscular arms as he put the boat in gear, eased it into the middle of the thin river, and took the thing along at a goodly pace. *Yep, much better.*

"So, feel like a date yet?" he asked, and her insides gave a hearty little wobble.

"This is textbook. In New York a date isn't really a date if there aren't wild animals involved."

And just like that she and Jonah North were officially on a date. And she was okay. Not deeper than her limits. Just…about…right. Feeling unusually content about her world and everything in it, Avery propped her feet on the dash; the wind whipping at her hair, the sun beating down on her nose, the deep rumble of the engine lulling her into a most relaxed state. Till the hum, and the heat, and *eau de Jonah* had her deep in memories of the night before.

"I hate to think what you're conjuring up over there, Ms Shaw."

She nearly leapt out of her skin. "Nothing. Just soaking it all in. Thinking."

"Dare I ask what about?"

To say it out loud would be pornographic. "I really liked your shack."

A surprised smile kicked up the corner of his mouth. "It's hardly the Waldorf."

"Why would you want it to be? It's unique. And cool. It suits you."

After a few beats, Jonah added, "It was my father's house."

"Were you brought up there?"

He nodded. "Never lived anywhere else." He frowned. "Not true. I spent three months in Sydney a few years back."

"You? In Sydney?" She was already laughing at the idea by the time she noticed the twitch in his jaw and the sense that the air temperature had slipped several degrees towards arctic. *Okay…* "Was it for work? Play? Sea change…in reverse?"

"My ex-fiancée lived there."

Well, she'd had to go and ask!

A deep swirly discomfort filled her up and she struggled

to decipher if her reaction was shock at the fact a woman had managed to put up with him for any length of time, or that she'd been wrong about his lone-wolfdom. There was a woman out there that this man had at one time been prepared to *marry*. A fiancée. *Ex*-fiancée, her subconscious shot quickly back.

"I'm assuming things didn't turn out so well," she said, her daze evident in her hoarse whisper.

But he was clearly caught up in thoughts of his own. She jumped a little when after some time he answered.

"She came here on holidays and stayed. Then she left. I followed. Got a position with a shipping company to manage their freight in and out of the harbour. Told myself water was water."

Clearly it hadn't been, as here he was. Mr Not Quite So Thoroughly Unattainable After All.

On a date.

With her.

"Wow," she croaked, "Sydney." Yep, she was focusing on the easier of the two shocks. "Try as I might I can't picture you living in the big smoke."

Storm clouds gathered in his eyes, his jaw so tight he looked liable to crack a tooth.

"Jonah—"

"Don't sweat it, Avery. You're not the first woman to think me provincial."

And *that* came from so far out of left-field Avery flinched. "Hold on there, partner, that's not what I meant at all. I'm sure you made a huge splash in Sydney."

"I didn't, in fact." He took the boat down a gear so that the change in engine swept his words clean away.

"Rubbish," she scoffed, imagining the looks on her friends' faces if she'd ever turned up with this guy on her arm. Those Manhattan blue bloods would take one look at those delicious eye crinkles, those big shoulders, and drop their jaws like a row of cartoon characters. And it wasn't just the way the guy looked—it was in his bearing, how obviously he lived his life to as high a standard as any man ever had. "I don't believe that for a second."

Jonah glanced up, the storm clouds parting just enough for a spark to gleam from within. A spark that met its twin in her belly.

"What I *meant*," she said, *now* choosing her words with care, "about me not being able to imagine you in *Sydney*, is that you seem like you were made for this place—the scorching sun, the squalling sea, the immense sky. Sydney would be a big grey blur in comparison. Which sounds ridiculous now I've put it into words—"

"No," Jonah said, frowning and smiling at the same time. "No."

"Okay." Avery hugged her arms around her belly to contain the tumbly feelings as they softened down to a constant hum. "So what happened with you and—"

"Rach? Real life."

"It has a way of getting in the way of things."

"You ever come close?" Jonah asked. "Marriage. Kids. The whole calamity."

"Me? No. Not unless you include Luke, of course, and he wasn't even aware of our impending plans."

Jonah laughed. An honest laugh. Confident, this man. Why wouldn't he be, though? Look at him. One hand resting casually on the wheel, a shoe nudged against the foot of the helm, eyes crinkling in the sunshine as he eased the boat around the reeded bends of the river.

This was a man who knew where he belonged.

The boat hit a wider stretch and Jonah slowed the engine to a throaty hum.

Maybe she still had to figure out where she really belonged. Not here. A ride on a dilapidated old boat at the top of Australia was probably a bit of a stretch considering where she'd come from. But here, so far away, made her realise how much of her life she spent trying to sort out her parents' lives. And the seed was now sown; to find her place. It would be hard. It would mean unravelling a decade's worth of ties before weaving them into something new. Something better.

Later, she thought as her throat began to constrict with the thought of it. Right now, the summer was hers. All hers. Nobody else's. And she no longer had any doubts about how she wanted to spend the time she had left.

Avery slipped off her stool and slipped under Jonah's arm, finding a perfect spot for herself between his knees. She rested a hand on his chest; the other took the cap from his head. His slow intake of breath and the darkening of his eyes created pools of heat low in her belly.

"So, Jonah North, what do you say we put all that behind us and just have some damn fun? No promises. No regrets. Do you want to be the man who makes my summer holiday one to remember?"

A muscle ticced in his jaw a moment before he grabbed her by the waist and drew her into him, covering her mouth with his. No finesse this time, no interminable teasing, just pure unleashed desire.

Lust rushed through her, unfettered, thick and fast, and she kissed him back, the heat of his mouth, the slide of his tongue driving every thought from her head but *more, now, yes*!

She threw his hat away—the man was hot but kissing a Sox fan would be sacrilege—and tucked her hands under his T-shirt, revelling in the warm skin, the rasp of hair, the sheer size of him. He was so big and hot and so much man he made her feel so light, like a breath of fresh air. As if nothing else mattered but here, now, this.

He tugged her closer, the ridge of his desire pressed

against her belly, and her head fell back as anticipation shivered through her with the surety of what was to come.

"What time do you have to have the boat back?"

Holding her close with one hand, Jonah grabbed his phone with the other, punched in a message, waited a long minute for a response, then with a wolfish grin said, "Never. The boat's mine."

Avery's knees near gave out. In her life she'd been wooed with bling, with tables at impossible-to-get-into restaurants, *never* had she had a man want her so much he'd bought the real estate under his feet in order to have her.

In one swift move he lifted her floaty top over her head, taking the hat with it. "Hell," he said, spying her bikini top which was made of mostly string a shade or two paler than her skin.

"You like? I found it in this wicked boutique in the Village—*oh...*"

Jonah proceeded to show her just how much he liked it by yanking it down to take her breast in his mouth. When she thought herself filled with more pleasure than she could possibly bear, his mouth slowly softened, placing gentle kisses over the moist tip.

And the thumb at her hip dipped below the beltline of her shorts. He found her button, snapped it open; the slide of her zip rent the quiet river air like a promise.

His hand slid an inch within. Her breath hitched, then he lifted his hand to run the backs of his knuckles over her stomach and her breath trembled out of her.

When his hand sank into the back of her shorts, the calloused pads of his palm cradling her backside with such gentleness, such reverence, she bit her lip to stop from crying out.

Using his teeth, he pulled the other half of her bikini top free, and took her nipple in his mouth, his tongue circling the tip but not quite touching. Right as his hand dived into her shorts and a finger swiped over her, once, then twice, then found her centre with the most perfect precision.

She gave in then, crying out. The crocodiles, wherever they might be, would just have to deal.

The gentle moans that followed sounded as if they were coming from a mile away but they were all her. Coming as they did with every slide of his finger, every lathe of his tongue.

Warmth spread through her, building to a searing heat where he touched, where he caressed, where he coaxed her higher, higher, till she reached a peak of insane pleasure. And there she stayed hovering, aching, for eons. And as she felt herself tip, as she began to spill over the other side he took her mouth, his tongue and touch guiding her all the way until she was left shaking in the strongest arms.

He held her there long after while she found herself gripped by mighty aftershocks. He pulled back only when she had stilled. Lifted her face with a finger to her chin, and kissed her. Eyes open. Such deep, absorbing eyes.

She reached between them, caressed the impressive length of him, wondering how on earth she'd coped with all that the night before. Her pulse quickened with anticipation at doing so again.

Grunting, he pulled his wallet from his back pocket, produced a small foil packet, which she snapped out of his grip. And with as much reverence as he'd shown her, she peeled away his pants and sheathed him, stopping every now and then for a sweet kiss, a swipe of her cheek, a lick.

With a growl he pulled her back upright, turned and backed her up against the dash. His eyes were like mercury, all slippery silver as he rid her of her bikini top and her shorts, leaving her naked.

The sun beat down on her shoulders, the dials dug into her back, and there was the occasional splash, the occasional bump of the hull, a possible deadly beast coming to say hello—but she didn't care.

All that mattered was Jonah, eyes roving over her as if he couldn't quite believe it. His hands followed, running over her so gently, tenderly, as if he was memorising her shape.

With a hand to his shoulder, she pulled him close, lifted a leg to hook around his hip, and then with a bone-deep sigh he was inside. Filling her slowly, achingly slowly, a sweet scrape that built till she couldn't stand it. He pulsed inside her, deeper, deeper, deeper than she'd ever been touched.

He came with a ferocity that made her head spin, and half a second later she followed right behind. Sensation imploding until all she could feel was the pulse between her legs. In her belly. In her heart. And Jonah's heart, thundering beneath her ear as she rested her head on his chest.

As they both struggled to drag in breaths, Jonah laughed, and Avery joined him. She lifted her head to find something fleeting and warming lighting his eyes.

Before she could pin it down he shook his head, hitched his shorts into place, then slumped back on the floor of the boat and lifted his face to the sun. "You're not the only one having a summer to remember, Miss Shaw."

Avery kneeled down to kiss him, then stood and spun about the boat butt naked. While Jonah lifted onto one elbow to watch, appreciation and wonder playing about his face.

And Avery wondered where she'd been her whole life.

Jonah took his time heading back.

One hand on the wheel, the other resting on Avery's lower back as she leant over the dash in her wild bikini top and short shorts. Sunlight flickering over her through the trees lining the marshy bank; her eyes otherwise cloaked in shadows from the brim of his ancient Akubra, her lush mouth tilted up at the corners.

It was so quiet out on the river, the scenery so rugged and raw they could have been the last two people on earth.

Then a telltale splash tugged at his instincts, and he squinted against the sun beating off the water. "Look," he said, his voice rough from under-use.

Avery blinked, followed the line of his arm, and saw. A croc. Its long brown body floating below the water snout, beady eyes, and a few bumpy scales cutting through the surface.

She stood taller, her fingers gripping the console till her nail beds turned bright pink. "It's huge."

"Twelve feet. Fourteen maybe."

She tipped back her hat—which had left a red mark slicing across her forehead. "It's looking right at me. No doubt thinking 'there's lunch.'"

"Don't blame him."

She flicked Jonah a glance, then licked her lips to cover a grin that made itself felt right in the groin. Then she turned, leant her backside against the dash, her long legs crossed at the ankles. "If, heaven forbid, I fell in right now you'd save me, right?"

"From a croc? Not on your life, princess. If he took you under that'd be it. They don't call it a death roll for nothing."

Her laughter was shocked, but the gleam in her eye was not. "How do the ladies resist you, Jonah North?"

"Resist me? Why do you think I let Hull skulk at my heels? Without him I'd be beating them away with a stick."

Her eyes narrowed a fraction, as if the idea of hordes of women coming after him was not one of her happier thoughts. "Ye-ea-a-ah," she said. "I actually half believe you. It's counterproductive, though, you know. Only adds to the tragic Heathcliffian mien you have going on."

"The what?"

"Nothing," she deadpanned.

Laughing under his breath, he ran a thumb along the red line on her forehead left by the hat. When her eyes flared at the touch, her breath hitching, her cheeks filling with blood, he tucked his hand back around the wheel.

His parents hadn't been demonstrative. Till then he'd figured he'd inherited the same. But the urge to touch Avery was strong. Too strong. So he did something he understood, reaching and slipping a hand around her waist, pulling her into the cradle between his legs.

His voice was rough as he said, "I notice Hull didn't scare you away."

"I notice you didn't beat me away with a stick."

The noticing beat between them like a pulse, until he pulled her in for a kiss. Her hand dived into the back of his hair, tugging till his skin thrummed with the sweet pleasure of her touch.

It took him longer than was smart to remember he was navigating croc-infested waters. He pulled away, thoughts all crooked. The intimacy part of this thing with Avery was so fresh, after keeping off every touch like an electric shock.

And yet he already found himself thinking towards the day her summer ended, while his simply kept on keeping on. Which was all he'd ever wanted. To belong here. In this paradise on earth. Where too much of a good thing was daily life.

The boat finally bumped against the riverbank back where they'd started, and Avery stretched away from him, yawning, leaving him to tie off. And get some space. Not that it seemed to help any. Her imprint lingered. Would do so for some time.

"Well, that was way more fun than I'd expected."

"Can I quote you for the website?"

The yawn turned into a grin. "Your slogan can be Satisfaction Guaranteed."

The tour operator called out a cheery welcome back, which stopped Jonah from giving her any kind of comeback. Leaving him to watch her head to the back of the boat to collect her stuff, her short shorts giving him a view of a hell of a length of leg.

She might have felt satisfied, but he felt as if his balls were in a vice.

The taste of her, the scent of her, the feel of her stamped on his senses like a brand. So much so he couldn't remember what any other woman of his experience felt like. Eyes on Avery, it was as if the rest had never existed.

But they did exist. And had taught him valuable life lessons. That things like this always ended. That advance bruise he felt behind his ribs was a good thing. Because this time he knew what was coming. This time it was in his control.

"Hull?" Avery said.

Yanked from his trance by the hitch in Avery's voice, Jonah looked past her to find Hull, not at the Jeep, but at the edge of the river, pacing back and forth so close to the edge his paws kept slipping into the water.

"Hey, boy," he called out. "No panic. We're back safe and sound." But Hull's whimpers only increased.

Jonah leapt off the boat the second he had it tied off. But instead of coming to sniff his hand Hull bolted to the Jeep, big paws clawing at the doors.

Flummoxed, Jonah looked to Avery, who hopped off the boat behind him and shrugged. He didn't know anything about dogs. He'd never had one as a kid—his father had never been home enough for it to be possible.

Jonah eased up to the dog, asked him to sit, which he did, which crazily made his heart squeeze. Then he ran gentle hands down Hull's legs, over his flanks, under his belly, checking to see if he might be hurt. Red-bellied black snakes liked water. Hull was tough. He'd survived being dumped. Survived where his brothers and sisters hadn't. He'd be fine.

"He doesn't look hurt to me," said Avery behind him. "He looks like he's pining."

"What?"

Avery's mouth twisted, then her eyes brightened. "Do you think he's found a lady friend?"

Jonah spun on his haunches, ready to shoot her theory down in flames. "He's three. A little over."

"That's twenty-one in dog years."

Jonah thought of himself at twenty-one and rocked back on his heels. "Aww hell."

"Unless of course he's neutered."

Jonah winced. "Hell, no!"

"Well, then, if your dog has knocked up some poor poodle, it's as much your responsibility as it is theirs."

"He's *not my dog*." But even as he said it he remembered the way he'd run after Hull into the forest the night before, panic like a fox trap around his chest. Thoughts catching on the burr of how blank his life would be without Hull in it. "You really think that's all it is?"

Avery snorted. "When the impulse can no longer be denied…"

Jonah's eyes swung back to the woman behind him. Her eyes liquid from the bright sun. Her clothes askew. Her skin pink from his stubble rash. Living proof of impulse no longer denied.

He looked back to his furry friend. "Hull." The dog looked up as he heard his name; all gentle eyes, wolfish profile, wildly speckled fur. "You missing your girl? Is that the problem?"

Hull licked his lips, panted, and Jonah swore beneath his breath. "What am I going to do with you, mate?"

Avery made snipping sounds that had Jonah clenching his man bits for all his might.

He whipped open the car door, and with a growl said, "Get in."

Hull leapt first, Avery followed.

Jonah took the keys back to the operator waiting in the hut, gave him Tim's card, and explained his man would get the lawyers together, then jogged back to the Jeep where a hot blonde and a hot-to-trot canine awaited him.

And he wondered at what point his well-managed life had gone to the dogs.

CHAPTER NINE

HALFWAY THROUGH AN early morning run up the beach path, Hull at his ankles, Jonah pulled up to jog on the spot. In the far distance he spied the ice-cream van that lived permanently on blocks in front of one of the dilapidated old beachfront homes that housed a half a dozen happy surfers.

Not that he felt like a half-melted ice cream. It was the blonde leaning into the thing that pulled him up short. Long lean legs, one bent so that her backside kicked out behind her, fair skin that had taken on the palest golden glow, long beach-waved hair trailing down her back.

Gone were the huge hat and fancy shoes that had been Avery's hallmark when she'd first arrived. In their place she wore the odd little fisherman's hat she'd picked up on Green Island and rubber thongs the local chemist sold for two bucks a pair. But the wild swimwear was all her—this one was strapless, the top a marvel of modern engineering, the bottom barely anything but a saucy frill that bounced as she lifted onto her toes to talk to the ice-cream guy who was now leaning out of the window, grinning through his dreadlocks.

And there but for the grace of God went he. Once upon a time *he'd* been one of those surfers who sat on that same porch, doing not much at all. It sounded nice in theory. Truth was it had been nice, and for a good while. Until it hadn't been enough.

Now he tried to carve an hour out of his work day every few weeks for a paddle, the way this kid no doubt carved an hour out of his surf time to put in an appearance at the dole office. The same kid who had all the time in the world to chat to a pretty tourist. And for the first time in years Jonah wondered who really had the better life.

Avery's laughter tinkled down the beach, and adrenalin poured through Jonah as he took off at a run.

She'd been in his bed near every day for the past week. Staying over more nights than not. And even while it was just a fling, Dreadlocks over there needed to know he wasn't in with a hope in hell. It was only neighbourly.

In fact *"just a fling"* had become somewhat of a mantra around his place, during those moments he found himself wondering when next he'd find her sitting at his kitchen table, draped in one of his shirts, one foot hooked up on a chair, hair a mussed mess as she smiled serenely out of the window at the forest-impeded ocean views beyond.

Unlike Rach, who'd set her treadmill up in his office, a small TV hooked to the front of it so she could watch the Kardashians, Avery soaked *every* moment in. Whether it was sitting on the jetty at Charter North watching him tinker with a dicky engine or on a bed of sketchy beach grass on Crescent Cove beach throwing a stick to Hull. She'd immersed herself in Crescent Cove.

Watching the cove through her eyes reminded him why he'd worked so hard to work himself back into the fabric of the place. And how little time he spent savouring it. What was the point of living in the most beautiful place on earth if you never even noticed?

Avery turned as he neared, hands wrapped around a cone. At the sight of her tongue curling about the melting ice cream, he missed a step and near ended up ass up. She looked up as he righted himself, grinned, and lifted her melting ice cream in a wave.

Hull peeled away to say hello and she crouched down to give the dog a cuddle about the ears. Even offered him a lick of the ice cream from her wrist and laughed when he took it.

When she stood Hull bounded back to join Jonah but from that point Avery's eyes were all on him as he jogged on the spot. He knew her odd eyes were dilated, even from the other side of the street. Knew they coursed over him, paused on the parts of him she liked best.

The urge to go to her, to kiss her, to throw her over his shoulder, and lock her up in his shack on the cliff was so thick, so all-encompassing, so *disquieting* he gave her a quick wave then kept running, just to prove he could.

"You!" said a woman who appeared as if from nowhere—her face red as a tomato.

Jonah only pulled up when he realised she wasn't talking to him, she was talking to Hull. "Ma'am, can I help you?"

"Don't you *Ma'am* me, sonny! Is this your dog?"

Jonah's cheek twitched with the urge to say no, but when Hull started whimpering in a way that made Jonah's insides go all squidgy, he heard himself say, "I'm his...main person."

"What the hell does that mean?"

It's all I've got for you, lady.

"Whatever you are, your...mongrel has been sniffing around my Petunia and you need to make him stop."

"Your—"

At that moment Avery appeared at his side. He caught her scent, her warmth, the zing of her travelling down his left arm before she even said a word.

"Hey, little thing. Petunia, is it?" she cooed, leaning towards the crazy woman's handbag where Jonah only just noticed a bald-headed little thing so overbred it could barely be labelled canine. Avery reached out to pat the thing's head, but it grew fangs and went in for a nip. She pulled back and sank down an arm around Hull's head, muttering loud enough for all to hear, "Really, Hull. Her?"

Jonah barely had a moment to note how much calmer Hull was with Avery all snuggled up to him before the woman stuck herself back into his line of sight. "Petunia is in heat."

Jonah snapped back to the present. "Do not tell me she's knocked up."

"No, she's not *carrying*! Thank goodness. And the last thing she needs is for your mutt to ruin her chances of producing champion offspring."

"My dog's not a mutt. While yours is—"

"Cute as a button," said Avery, standing at his side. "And champion, hey? Wowee. If she was my dog I'd take extra special care to keep her away from lusty male suitors. They can be temptation incarnate when they're all big and hairy like this guy."

Her voice was so kind, consoling, with that sophisticated New York measure, that the woman's face twitched as though she had a glitch in her regular programming. Then her eyes slid away from Avery and back to Jonah. And she looked at him as if she hadn't really seen him before. More precisely, looked hard at his big and hairy chest.

Jonah took a step back and the woman shook her head as if coming out of a trance. "Just keep your mutt on a leash. Or I'll sue. Or I'll have him put down."

At that Jonah regained his lost step and more, leaning in and forcing the woman to look up and up and up. "Hang on a second, lady. If you kept your Pansy—"

"Petunia," Avery muttered.

"Petunia—*whatever*—at home while she's in heat rather than schlepping her out in your bloody handbag, then my dog wouldn't have looked twice at her. And I'll have you know he's not a mutt. He's a superb dog. A smart dog. A loving, loyal, kind dog. You and your little rat would be lucky to have him in your life!"

The other woman stormed off with her shivering critter in tow.

"Wow," Jonah said, running a hand over his sweat-dampened hair, knowing not all the sweat had been from the running. He glared down at Hull, who looked up at him with a kind of despair as the object of his affection was whisked away.

"Your dog."

Jonah glanced at Avery to find her back to licking her ice cream, a rogue smile gleaming deep within her mismatched eyes.

"I'm sorry?"

"You said Hull was *your* dog. There's no going back from that."

She tipped up onto her toes, placed a cool hand on his bare chest, and kissed him, a seriously hot lip lock that tasted like summer and ice cream and everything sweet and wholesome. Everything about the cove that made it feel like home. Then her hand trailed down his chest, her nails catching in his chest hair in a way that was the opposite of wholesome.

She walked backwards, back towards the resort, the frill of her bikini bottom bouncing up and down as if it were beckoning him to follow. Then said, "Your dog's a big softie, Jonah North. Just like his owner."

"Didn't I just hear you tell that woman I was temptation incarnate?"

She didn't even pretend she was talking about Hull. "I'm in PR. Which more often than not means taking not naturally pleasant products and talking them up till they smell like roses. Now you know I'm good at it."

Hips swinging, hair swaying, cheap thongs slapping on the hot concrete, she left him feeling anything but soft.

With a growl he turned and ran. And ran. And ran.

* * *

Avery headed into the Tropicana Nights, all aglow after her little run-in with Jonah.

Intending to take a long cool shower to wash off the sunscreen and ice cream and smirk before checking in with her mother, she took a short cut past the pool. Middle of the day and there was nobody there. So she gave her sticky hands a quick wash in the crystal-clear pool, then nearly fell in when she saw she wasn't alone—Claudia was all curled up on a white sun lounge.

"Hey, stranger!" Avery called out as she neared.

Claudia came to as if from far away. "Hey, kiddo! What's the haps?"

Avery parked her backside in the lounge next to Claudia's and filled her in on the unlikely Petunia.

"So you and Jonah are getting along quite well, then," Claude asked.

"We are," said Avery, and even she heard the sigh in her voice. So she qualified, "I mean, if you could create the perfect man for a summer fling, he'd be it, right?"

Claudia nodded wistfully. "Can't fault your logic there."

Avery nudged Claude's chair with her foot. "Which is why it kind of shocks me that he was *engaged* once upon a time."

"That he was," Claude said, the nods slowing. "Are you digging?"

"Frantically," Avery admitted.

"Her name was Rachel."

"Got that."

"She lived here, with him, for several months."

Months? Several?

"She was gorgeous, too. Uber-tanned, luscious dark hair, legs that went on forever. Amazonian, really. Like a half-foot taller than you. Fitness freak too, a body that would make you weep. And charismatic! Reserves of energy like nobody I've ever met—"

"Right, okay," Avery said, leaning over and slamming a hand over Claude's now-laughing mouth. "I get it. She was perfect."

Claude ducked away, grin intact. "She was a cool chick. But she was totally wrong for Jonah."

"How?" she asked, wondering how much it had to do with her being a city girl, him being a beach boy. Wishing she didn't care about the answer so very much.

"Turned out she was only waiting out her time here till her boss back in Sydney offered up a big enough package to lure her back."

"But weren't they engaged?"

"I think she'd have happily taken him back to Sydney and kept him there if he didn't do that big, strong, tree man thing better than any man I've ever known. She never saw beyond the hotness and the stubbornness to his big heart." Claude's eyes narrowed a fraction, then she said, "You see it, though, don't you?"

"What?" Well, sure she did, but that was beside the point. "No. Don't you go getting ideas now."

"I had to try."

"Wouldn't be you if you didn't."

Claudia took Avery's hands and squeezed, as if making sure Avery was paying attention before she said, "You need to know, though, that I've never seen him smile as much as when he's with you. While you..." Claude's eyes roved over Avery's face. "You, my friend, are glowing."

Avery flapped a "shut up" hand at Claude, and lay back in her sun lounge. Staring up at the cloudless blue sky, more questions came to her only when she looked over at Claude it was to find tears streaming down her face. She leapt to Claude's sun lounge, wrapping an arm about her shoulder. "Claude! Are they happy tears? Tell me they're happy tears!"

Claudia perked up, swiped under her eyes, and smiled. It was a pathetic effort. At least now her friend might be ready to tell her what the hell was really going on.

"That's it," Avery said, "enough of this stoic crap. Tell me. Are your parents okay?"

Claude shook her head so hard her wispy ponytail slapped her in the cheeks. "No, nothing like that. It's just while you're having the best summer of your life I can safely say this has been my worst. The resort… You must have noticed how quiet we are."

Avery looked across the vast pool that curled beneath the balconies of dozens of empty rooms. "When I said I was coming you said something about renovating, so I just thought—"

Claudia laughed, and sniffed. "We can't renovate. We have no money. The resort's bust, or near enough. I've been scraping by since I took over, but so much needs fixing and there's nothing left to fix it."

"Why didn't you tell me all this before?"

"Because I wanted you to have a good time. And I'm pissed off at my parents for not being here to give me any advice. And now I just don't know what else I can do."

Avery's stomach turned at the fear in Claudia's big blue eyes. "Luke's the advertising guru, right? What plans has he put in place?"

"Robot just sent me an email," Claude said, flashing her phone at Avery before curling it back into a tight grip. "He's given me an ultimatum. Get the resort in the black or he's taking over."

"What?"

"He wants to turn it into some flashy Contiki-style resort with a swim-up bar, and toga parties catering to hordes of drunken twenty-somethings."

"He does not!"

"He has figures, graphs, a business plan."

"But that's not what the Tropicana Nights is about. It's kitsch. Family fun. Like a cruise ship without the sea-sickness."

"Yes! You get it and you've only been here twice. He grew up here and still—" She couldn't get the words out.

"What an ass," Avery said.

And Claude coughed out a laugh. Her laughter turned to more tears, but it was better that than staring into space as she had been the past minute. "Wasn't this the same man you were set to ride off into the sunset with not that long ago?"

"I saw the error of my ways just in time."

"Thank goodness for Jonah."

Yeah, thank goodness for Jonah. But she didn't have time for that now. In fact she'd been a horrible friend all summer, letting Claude get this far without bringing her into the loop.

Avery took Claude by the arms and gave her a shake. "What do you need me to do?"

"You can't do anything."

"I can do quite a lot, as it turns out. I didn't get a first-class education for nothing."

"There's no time."

"Not for a complete turnaround, sure. But what if we could stall Luke? To convince him to give you a stay of execution?"

A flicker of hope came to life in Claude's eyes. "But you're busy."

"Doing what?"

"Jonah."

"Funny girl."

Claude gave a watery smile.

"Claude, I'm not about to walk away from you for some

hot summer loving. You're family." *And family comes first.* How many times had her mother said that, using it as a hook to drag Avery back into the fold any time she looked ready to stray? This time it was true.

Claude's mouth flashed into its first full smile. "Is it as hot as I imagine?"

"Hotter. And yet, here I am. What do you need?"

Sighing long and hard as her glassy gaze wafted over the huge, near-empty resort surrounding them all sides, Claude admitted, "A miracle."

"A party," Jonah repeated as Avery used his warm bare chest as a pillow. Together they lay on a massive hammock strung between two leaning palm trees down on his secluded private beach at the base of his cliff while the tide lapped a lullaby against the big black rocks cradling the small patch of sand.

"Not just a party," Avery said on a blissful sigh. "*The* party. I'm a New Yorker, Mr North. One who has spent nearly every August of my life in the Hamptons. My mother is on so many charity boards it would make you wince. And I am quite the PR savant. So I, Mr North, *know* how to throw a party."

Ironic, considering a party was why she'd fled her home country in the first place. Another reason why the party to relaunch the Tropicana Nights Resort was going to be the most upbeat party ever thrown.

"And it's you, young Jonah, who gave me the idea."

"I seriously doubt that," he murmured, his deep voice reverberating through her chest.

"Way back when, you told me the cove was more than a tourist town—it's a real community. I figured, why not let that community rally around the idea of an 'under new management' icon? So we've invited everyone who has any influence on where people stay in this town. And, using one of the great secrets of the human condition, we'll make them desperate to come by charging an absolute packet for tickets, thus giving Claude's coffers an immediate boost! We are going to put the Tropicana Nights Resort back on the map."

He lifted his head and cupped her chin so he could look her in the eye, clearly less excited than Claude had been. "So what you're really telling me is that you'll be busy the next couple of weeks."

Oh, that's why. "Some."

"Hmm," he growled, lowering himself back down. And wrapping her up tighter. She was near sure of it.

And even while every inch of her craved nothing more than to spend every second of her summer she had left in the arms of this man—converting him to her beloved Yankees—Go Yanks!—watching him let himself love Hull, and just swimming deep in the tumble of feelings she'd never come close to feeling before, Claude was her oldest friend.

And thus, miles from home, she'd once again found herself caught in the perennial tug of war between responsibility and aspiration.

In the past responsibility won, every time. It wasn't even a question. She'd lost count of the dates she'd broken because her mother had called her on her way to a nervous breakdown. But far from the epicentre of that life, she could see that she'd been perfectly happy to indulge in her mother's emotional blackmail. The ready excuse had been a *relief.* Beneath the Pollyanna effervescence, she'd been paralysed by fear of getting hurt.

But here, now, for the first time in memory she felt as if the choice was totally up to her. And while helping Claude in her time of greatest need was a no-brainer, she was all in with Jonah for as long as she had him.

"I'll be busy," she said, shuffling till she fell deeper into his grooves. "But not all the time."

Getting her meaning loud and clear, Jonah ran a lazy finger up and down her bare back, making her spine curl.

"In fact, I foresee many more days like this before my time here is at an end."

His hand stopped its delicious exploration as she felt him harden beneath her, and not in a good way. She shifted to look at his face to find the muscles in his jaw working overtime and his eyes glinting with silver streaks.

She took a careful breath, and had even more careful thoughts. They didn't ever talk about her leaving, but only because they hadn't needed to. It was simply there, a big beautiful prophylactic against the times she found her softer self wondering if being "all in" was less about time and more about the connection between them. Those moments when she caught him looking at her in a way that made her feel something sweet and painful, when it bloomed so sudden and bright within her it took her breath away.

Needing to change the subject, Avery said, "Speaking of hammocks."

"Were we?"

"Yes," she said, waiting for him to agree to pretend they hadn't both been thinking about The End.

With a short expulsion of breath he nodded. "Hammocks."

"Can we borrow yours?"

"For what?

"The party! Have you not been listening to a word I've said?"

"Hard when you keep wriggling against me like that."

This they could do, Avery thought, curving her spine to meet his hand, breathing out long and hard when it went back to its lazy trawls up and down her back. The sexy stuff left little room for thinking, much less over-thinking.

"That's not the only way you're going to help, either," she said, running a hand over his pecs, his beautiful brown skin rippling under her palm.

"Who said I was going to help at all?"

"I did. You are buying tickets for the entire Charter North office. And I've already messaged Tim a list of the boating decor you'll be loaning us for the evening."

The sexy touching stopped as he moved to glare into her eyes. She wondered how she'd ever found that look infuriating. It was seriously hot. "You sidestepped me to go through Tim?"

"He's nicer than you are. He doesn't argue. He compliments me on my shoes. I think he likes me more than you do too."

"Not possible," he said without thinking, and the bittersweet bloom of feelings inside her ratcheted up to cyclonic levels. "He's gay, you know. Tim. Has a boyfriend. Going on three years now."

"Fabulous. Buy the boyfriend a ticket too."

At that Jonah laughed—finally!—the glare easing to a gleam. Then, by way of an answer, he kissed the corner of her mouth, then the other one, with a gentleness that the gleam in his eyes concealed. Grouchy Jonah was hot, but gentle Jonah, the one who snuck up on her at the least expected moments, was the one who could tear her apart.

She'd miss him when she left—more than it bore thinking about—but she'd never regret leaping into the wild wonderful world of Jonah North. And *that*, she decided in a brilliant epiphany, was the key. It wasn't the looming sense of loss that would define life after this summer, but how she dealt with it. She would not feel sorry for herself. She would not harp on it. And life would go on.

She pulled back to trace the bump on his nose, the ridge

of his cheekbone, the crinkles at the edge of an eye. His skin was so hot, so real.

Jonah's eyebrow raised in question.

Since she knew the surest way to have him leaping from the hammock and running for his life was to give him any indication what was going through her head, she scored her hands through his hair, his glorious dark curls, and drew his mouth back to hers. And with the ocean clawing its way onto the beach below, the sun baking the earth around them, she kissed him till she felt nothing but him. But this. All this.

For now...

Later that evening, curled up in a big round cane chair on Jonah's back porch, Avery found herself thinking more and more about home. Wondering if the best thing to do would be to book her flight back so that it was done.

Instead—as if *that* were the lesser of two evils—she Skyped her mother. She'd been avoiding it all week. Ever since she and Claude had started organising the party, in fact. Because it would come up. And then so would the *other* party. And distraction and avoidance had worked brilliantly so far, so why mess with it?

By the time her mother answered—her neat ash-blonde bob and perfectly made-up face flitting onto the screen—Avery's throat was so tight she wondered if she'd get a word out at all.

Lucky her mother was on song. "Who are you and what have you done with my daughter?"

Avery glanced at the small version of herself in the bottom of the screen, and realised for the first time since she'd arrived it hadn't occurred to her to dress up for the call. She had shaggy beach hair, freckles on her nose, wore a bikini and nothing else.

But that wasn't why she couldn't drag her eyes away

from her own image. Her mouth was soft. Her shoulders relaxed. Her eyes content. Somehow in the past few weeks she'd shed her air of quiet desperation and she looked… happy.

The tapping away of a computer keyboard in the office behind the open window farther down the porch brought her back to the present.

Blinking, she dragged her gaze back to the main screen. "You hate the tan, right?"

Caroline Shaw—she'd kept her ex-husband's name— rolled her eyes, careful not to wrinkle. "So long as you're using sunscreen. And moisturiser. And toner. And—"

"I'm having a fabulous time, thanks for asking."

When her mother smiled at the hit, Avery went on to fill her in on the happenings around the cove—about Claude, and Isis and Cyrus, and Hull and his lady friend. Not about the party, though. Or the man taking up most of her time.

"What about that man?" her mother asked, glancing away to grab a china cup hopefully filled with tea as Avery jumped.

It took everything in her power now to glance towards the glow of Jonah's window as she asked, "What man?"

"The hotelier. We came to know his parents all those years ago."

"The… *Luke*?"

"Mmm. I Googled him when you brought him up at one time. Handsome fellow. Eminently eligible. Divorced," she said with the usual hiss that implied, "but redeemable, one might hope. You haven't mentioned him in a while so I wondered, if perhaps…"

Avery had forgotten that her mother was like a human tuning fork, trembling in aggravation any time she thought her only daughter might be cast aside by some evil man as she herself had once been.

It would have been easy to pretend, just as it had been

easier to walk away from every romantic relationship than to think about why that was. But, for the first time in re-callable history, she said to her mother: "No. I'm actually seeing someone else."

Her mother paused with the teacup halfway to her mouth. "And who is this lucky young man?"

Avery's heart beat hard as she watched her mother's every facial movement for signs of a meltdown. "His name is Jonah. He's a local. We met in the ocean. Hull—the dog with the lady-friend—is his."

Good grief. Could she have offered a less interesting version of the man? But this was a watershed moment and she was doing her best.

"As handsome as the other one?" her mother asked gently as if she knew that Avery was struggling not to gush.

"More."

Her mother smiled softly, sadly, and Avery suddenly wished she hadn't said anything at all. Dealing with her mother as she raged at the world was one thing, seeing her wistful was like a knife to the heart.

Avery heard the shower start up, meaning Jonah was done with whatever he'd been working on in his office and was getting ready for bed. This *handsome* man she was seeing. Hearing it inside her head she saw how vanilla that sounded, how weak a description for what had happened to her this summer.

And she felt with a sharp keening deep inside her how little of that summer was left.

She feigned a yawn.

Her mother attempted to raise an eyebrow, which, considering the years of Botox, was a near impossibility. "Sleepy, darling? You'd be heading out now if you were back here."

The idea of heading out paled into insignificance compared with what was awaiting her by staying in. "Life's different here. It's slower. Gentler. It revolves around the sun. It's..." This time she couldn't stop herself glancing towards the window down the way, the light spilling out onto the rough wood and mixing with the unimpeded moonlight. "It's curative."

When Avery looked back at her mother's image on the screen, it was to find her mouth open, her forehead pinched, as if she was about say something; something Avery wouldn't like. Avery's stomach clenched. *Please*, she begged silently, not sure what she was pleading for. Time? Understanding? Amnesty? Release...?

Then her mother said, "Love you, baby girl. Take care. Come home soon." And signed off.

Avery breathed out hard.

She put Jonah's tablet on the kitchen bench inside and padded into his bedroom to find his en-suite shower—hot the way he liked it, filling both rooms with steam. And the man himself stripping bare.

Her eyes trailed his beautiful form, the movement of muscles across his back, the perfect pale backside between the deep golden-brown of his back and his thighs, like a hint of sweetness amidst all that raw testosterone.

She went to him and ran a hand over each cheek, kissing her way across his shoulder blades, grinning against him as his muscles clenched deliciously at her touch.

"You all done out there?" he asked, turning, his scrunched up T-shirt warm and soft between them.

"Mmm-hmm," she said, trailing fingers over the bumps of his biceps.

"All good?" he asked, his voice tight.

She glanced up to find his eyes were dark. His energy reined in. She couldn't wait for the moment it wasn't.

"As good as can be expected. My mother did wonder one thing..."

"What's that?"

"She wondered why I wasn't planning on going out."

"What did you tell her?"

"We're close, but we're not that close." With that she lifted onto her toes, sank her hands into his hair, and kissed him, melting from the outside in when he dropped the T-shirt and held her, his naked heat against her bikini-clad skin.

Lifting her lanky self into his arms as if she weighed nothing at all, he walked her into the bathroom, and dumped her in the shower, her head right under the hot spray. Laughing, she pushed her hair out of her eyes and grinned up at him. The grin fading to a sigh, when she caught the heat in his eyes.

Curative, she thought as he enfolded her in his strong arms, and kissed her till she saw stars. Making her wonder just what Jonah North might be curing her of.

CHAPTER TEN

AVERY NEVER DID get the chance to book that plane ticket home as the next week and a half of her life was consumed by the organising of The Party.

Claude had picked the theme—*Beyond the Sea.* Leaving room for exactly the kind of kitsch fun of the Tropicana Nights she had in mind along with a hefty dose of glamour, elegance, and old-world nostalgia, Avery Shaw style.

Dean Martin crooned smoothly beneath the sounds of laughter and chatter of the guests. Champagne, locally brewed beer, and pineapple punch flowed, served by a cute-as-a-button mermaid and a total hottie merman. Frangipani flowers and silver tea lights floated in the pool and above it all hung a web of lobster nets from which glinted strings of pure white fairy lights.

Jonah—by way of Tim the office manager—had donated the nets, life-preservers for the wait staff, and life rings for decorations, and the dozen vintage rum barrels currently serving as occasional tables. But the yacht? That was pure Jonah. A gorgeous black and silver thing reposing with lazy elegance on stumps in one corner of the pool deck, it had arrived at the resort the day before, complete with a crane to put it into place. There'd been no word as to where it had come from, just a note: "Raffle it. Knock 'em dead, kiddo." From the raffle tickets alone Claude had already made enough money to keep the resort afloat for a month.

Claudia leaned her head on Avery's shoulder as they took a rare breather from hostess duties. "I couldn't afford to throw a beach ball much less a party, but look at this."

Avery lifted her beer bottle in salute. "And this is only the beginning. Once the travel bloggers start trickling in for their free stays word will really get out that you offer something really special here, Claude. And people will come."

"I don't know how I can do all that without you, Avery."

Avery held her hand. Hard.

She'd always thought her attraction to PR was a natural extension of all those years playing Pollyanna with her mom and dad. But standing there with her best friend in the whole world, seeing their efforts about to come to fruition, felt pretty different from… What had she said to Jonah? *Taking not naturally pleasant products and talking them up till they smelled like roses.*

Avery drew Claude's arm close. "Go mingle. Thank. Drum up clients. A hotelier's work is never done."

Claudia pulled herself up straight, and went to do just that.

Which was when Avery felt a hand land on her lower back. She knew instantly it didn't belong to Jonah—no spark, no warmth, no drizzle of sensation that hit the backs of her knees and stayed even after his touch was gone.

She spun to find Luke—clean-shaven, neat as a pin, resplendent in his slick suit.

"Luke!" She leaned in and kissed his cheek. "Wow. No tie. It must be a party. Does Claude know you're here? She'll be thrilled you made it back in time to see her glory unfold."

"Sure about that?"

"Absolutely. And this is only a taste of the kinds of ideas

she has going forward. So you need to cut our girl some slack or you'll have me to deal with. Don't even think I'm kidding. I'm a New Yorker, remember. I know people."

Luke tapped the side of his nose. "I'll take it into consideration. Where is she?"

"She was heading to... Oh."

Avery caught sight of Claudia's wispy blonde ponytail. She was dancing with a dark-haired, dark-eyed, snake-hipped man who held her very, very close. It could only be Raoul.

Avery turned to Luke to point her out. By the look in Luke's eyes she didn't need to.

Tunnel vision down to an art form, Luke said, "Nice to see you, Avery," then made a beeline for his business partner.

Avery made to follow, to play intermediary, till she felt a pair of hands encircle her waist from behind, and this time there was no doubting who they belonged to. She leant into Jonah's warmth, sighing all over as she sank into his touch.

"How's Luke?" he asked in that deep, sexy, *sexy* voice of his.

"Had you worried there, did I?"

"Not for a New York second."

"A New York second, eh? You do know that's like a tenth the length of a Crescent Cove second."

"You're really going there?" His tone was joking, but the dark thread wavering beneath it curled itself around Avery's heart and pulled tight. But the thing was, the time was coming when she *would* be going there. They couldn't avoid it forever.

Beer, adrenalin, and the fact that she wasn't looking into his eyes gave her the guts to say, "Afraid you'll miss me so desperately when I go?"

He sank a kiss into her hair, his lips staying put. "No point. Without me around the moment you get home you'll fall down a sewer hole and never be seen again. And then I'll have to console Claudia. She'll insist we build a memorial. And I'm a busy man, don't you know?"

She knew. And she also knew how much time he'd carved out for her these past few weeks. The late starts, the early afternoons, the long delicious nights. Avery's stomach clenched so hard she put a hand on her belly. Jonah's hand landed quietly over the top. And there they stayed a few minutes, simply soaking in one another's warmth.

Then Jonah's chin landed on her shoulder, his breath brushing her ear. "Ms Shaw, are you actually drinking a beer?"

Avery lifted the bottle to her mouth and took a swig. Jonah growled in appreciation.

"I'd have thought you'd like women with a bit of tomboy in them. Women who can hoist a rigging. And swing an anchor. And lift a… No. I'm done."

There was a beat, like a moment lost in time, before he murmured, "I like you."

And while Avery's heart near imploded, she somehow managed to say, "Took your sweet time."

He laughed, the *huh-huh-huh* tripping gorgeously down her arms, before casual as you please he unwound his arms and ambled away.

Avery's breath shuddered through her chest as she stared after him. Watching him ease through the multitude, stopping to chat whenever anyone called his name. Such a man. A *good* man, she thought, her gaze glancing off all the extras he'd donated without having been asked. The yacht he'd given simply because he could. No fanfare. No drama. Just honest, down-to-earth decency.

And this man *liked* her.

She liked him too. She felt full around him—light and safe and important. She felt desired. She felt raw. In fact she liked the Avery she was around him. The one who didn't have to try so hard all the time.

The sexy, pulsing thrum of The Flamingos' "I Only Have Eyes For You" hummed from the speaker near Avery's feet. A burst of laughter split the night from somewhere to her right. A drip of condensation slid from the cold beer bottle clasped gently in her grip to land on her foot.

As just like that, between breaths, between beats, between one second and the next, Avery Shaw fell in love for the first time in her life.

Jonah watched Avery laughing it up with Tim and his boyfriend, Roger. Playing referee between Luke and Claude. Mesmerising the ice-cream-van guy and the rest of the Dreadlock Army who'd managed to wangle tickets from who knew where—though by the number of nubile young female tourists fluttering around them it had probably been a smart move to bus them in.

Not that he did any more than notice the others. Not with the way Avery seemed to fill his vision. Her dress a shimmery cream concoction of ruffles that made her skin gleam. Her hair a shining waterfall down her back. String of tiny silver beads sparkled on her wrist throwing off light every time she moved.

And it took every bit of self-restraint he had not to drag her away and find somewhere quiet, somewhere private, even if just to mess her up some.

Instead he downed a goodly dose of beer.

For these feelings were not fun. They were bloody terrifying. For this Avery wasn't the one he knew. In her place was some kind of professional miracle worker. What she'd done in whipping the slow-moving folk of the cove into a near frenzy to throw the bash of the century in such a short space of time was nothing short of miraculous.

She was something else—not that *his Avery* hadn't tried to tell him as much on many an occasion: competitive swimmer, life spent travelling the world, PR whiz in what was no doubt the toughest market in the world, with a life bigger, brighter, snazzier than he could possibly know.

Like knocking on a brick wall with a feather, it had been. Because he hadn't wanted to see it. Preferring to focus on her futile resistance to his charms. How readily she'd made room for him in her life. The ease with which she'd fitted into his. And how, for the first time in a half-dozen years, he'd found a reason big enough to carve time away from his business.

But tonight there was no hiding from the stark reality before him.

The Avery who'd snuck under his skin, made herself right at home, who looked as if she were born in a bikini, was at her heart a social butterfly, a Park Avenue Princess. She *glowed* out there, under the bright lights and attention.

While at his very essence he was a beach bum who'd had no plans beyond living off his father's meagre life insurance until a kick in the pants had brought his life to the very crux of survival.

Like a hard tug on the cord of an abandoned outboard motor, that resting survival instinct coughed and spluttered back to life, and Jonah took a step back, near tripping over a vintage rum barrel. One of his. Collector's items; he'd seen them, wanted them, and just had to have. So he'd made them his.

An offshoot of thriving so stridently. He'd become cocky. Proven by the fact that he'd seen Avery, wanted her, and hadn't let anything stand in the way of having her. Not the fact that she was a tourist. Not the fact that she drove him around the bend. Not even when her ridiculous notion of Luke had given him the best possible out.

All signs he'd ignored; when Avery and her kisses and

sweet skin and nothing to do but him were gateway drugs back to the old days. When he'd taken pleasure for pleasure's sake. When he'd had no responsibilities. When he'd had nobody left in his life to set him any boundaries. When things had felt simple, and easy, and free.

As if she'd sensed him watching, whatever she'd been saying came to a halt. Her cheeks pinked as her eyes lit on his and sparkled. She lifted the beer in salute. And by the time someone stepped in between them, blocking her from view, Jonah's lungs felt as if they were filling with water.

Avoiding the rum barrel, Jonah turned and walked away. Stopping only when he found a place he could think straight. He found it amongst the girls from the Tea Tree Resort of Green Island. They clearly didn't care that he didn't join in their conversation, which was something about men in boots.

Charming girls, he thought, their familiar accents earthing him. Charming like the cove. But the cove was too far away from the rest of the world to hold any but the most determined, the most dug in, forever. Avery would go back where *she* belonged and he'd be left rattling around in his big house. His big life. His full life.

A life that had felt like more than enough.

Until he'd gone looking for something he felt was missing that fateful morning, and found Avery.

His survival instincts were roaring now, propelling him fast and hard in the right direction. The other stuff, the stuff he didn't want to think about any more, he shut down piece by piece.

It was a trick he'd learnt after his mother had left. A trick he'd utilised, every night after, waiting past dark for his father to come home, never entirely sure that he would. Until the night he'd not come home at all.

In that state of numbed relief he'd remain. At least until the day Avery Shaw finally flew out of his life. And then, as before, he'd claw his way back out, using the restorative air of his home to bring him back to life again.

It was near three in the morning when Avery made it back to the Tiki Suite and floated inside, the gratification of success, a couple of late cocktails with an ebullient Claudia, and the wild blow of feelings for Jonah giving her wings.

She wished he were there to help her work off her adrenalin, but he'd disappeared at some point around midnight. Once the girls from Green Island had imbibed enough cocktails to start following him around and calling him Captain Jack, she'd known he'd only last so long.

Instead she decided to call her mother. It would be the afternoon before the other party. The flipside. Evil to Avery's Good. Even as it made her tummy flutter, it would be heartless not to let her mother know she was thinking about her, hoping it went…not disastrously. So why not do so while she was full of beer and joy?

Lying on her bed, moonlight pouring through the window, she pressed the phone to her ear.

"Hey," Avery said when her mother answered, her voice croaky from all the *talking, talking, talking.*

"Darling," her mother said, her voice so weary Avery quickly checked her phone to make sure she hadn't got the time wrong. "What time is it there?"

"Middle of the night. But that's okay. I'm just home from a party Claude and I threw. A Tropicana reboot. And it was fabulous."

"I have no doubt."

Avery swallowed. "Are you all ready for yours?"

"Hmm?"

"Your party?"

"Oh. Didn't I mention…? I cancelled it."

Didn't she…? *What?* Wow! And no. But good, right? Maybe even a breakthrough! The very idea of which swam through Avery like a wave of hope, of possibility that maybe things were changing on both sides of the world—

"Are you sitting down?" her mother asked, breaking into her reverie.

"Um, sure," Avery lied, lifting up onto her elbow at least.

"I have some news I was hoping to save until your return, but I don't want you to hear it on the grapevine, so... Darling, your father's getting remarried."

Avery's elbow shot out from under her.

"Darling?"

"I heard." Avery dragged herself to sitting, leaning forward over her crossed legs, the back of a hand on her suddenly spiking-hot forehead. Her father...getting remarried? "Oh, Mom."

"You seemed so happy when we Skyped last week, so content, I couldn't... But you had to know some time, so there it is. Phillip's getting *married*," her mother said again, and this time Avery heard more than just the words. She heard the deep quiet, the gentle sorrow, the *fresh* heartbreak. *Oh, Mom.* "Are *you* okay?"

"I'll be fine. Aren't I always?"

Avery could have begged to differ, but she let that one lie. Saying no to her mother was a lesson she had to learn, but that was not the time.

"Maybe this is a good thing..." Avery offered up, feeling sixteen all over again as she squeezed her eyes shut tight. "Maybe now you can move on."

"Sweet girl," said Caroline, making no promises.

And for the first time since their family fell apart, Avery kind of understood. There was a fine line between love and...not *hate* so much as exasperation. Avery knew how that felt. Jonah had taken her there these past weeks, right to the tipping point and back again, with his stubbornness, self-assuredness, neutrality. How long it had taken for him to even admit he *liked* her?

It was a scary thing, the tipping. But the reward so was worth it. Every time she saw in his eyes and felt in his touch that what was happening between them was so much bigger than *"like."*

Maybe that was why her mother had hung on as long as she could. Not out of some kind of predisposition to hysteria, but because when it had been good it had been beyond compare.

Avery bit her lip to stop the emotion welling up inside her.

"Darling," said her mother, into the silence, "just this one last thing. Something to tuck away for one day. When you find the one it's not all hearts and flowers—it's two separate people trying to fit into one another's lives. Which can feel nearly impossible at times. But no matter how hard it might be to live with them, it's far harder to live without them."

One day? Avery thought. Wondering if across the miles her mother had a single clue that her *one day* was *this day.* So much philosophy from her mother to take in at three in the morning, Avery pressed her fingers to her eyes.

"Now, just forget about it. Go back to enjoying your holiday. Is it sunny there?"

Avery looked at the moonlight shaving swathes into the darkness. "Sunny like no place on earth."

"Cover up. Hats and sunscreen. Don't ruin that gorgeous skin of yours. You're only young once. Blink and it's gone."

That was when the tears came. Big fat ones that left a big wet patch on her party dress.

"Love you, Mom."

"Love you too, baby girl."

Avery hung up her phone and held it in her lap. Shoulders hunched, she looked out at the moonlit sky. The same moon that would rise over New York the next night.

She imagined herself standing outside JFK airport, icy wind slapping her coat against her legs, the sharp scent of the island making her nostrils flare, the sound of a million cabs fighting for space.

Shaking her head she replaced the view with the angel in Central Park, with the stairs of the New York Public Library, with her favourite discount shoe shop deep in the canyons of the financial district. The colour of Broadway. Her favourite cocktail bar in the Flatiron. Laughing with her friends, sharing stories about people they all knew, had known all their lives.

She blinked and suddenly saw Jonah's face, his eyes crinkling, white teeth flashing in his brown face, his dark curls glistening with ocean water, sun pouring over his skin. She closed her eyes on a ragged sigh and felt his hand on her waist, sliding over her ribs, scraping the edge of her breast. She opened her mouth to his taste. His heat. His desire.

And his difference. Everyone took Avery at face value. Happy go lucky. Always with the smiling. With Jonah she'd never been anything but herself. Good, bad. Delighted, irate. Whatever that was at any given moment.

And her heart clenched with such a beat of loneliness, a foreshadowing of what she'd be—who she'd be—without him in her life.

Because she'd soon find out.

Her mother might be putting on a brave face, but, for all the drama of the past decade, this would be the hardest thing she'd gone through. And Avery had to be there. Not to do cartwheels and tell her everything was going to be okay. But to give her mother a hug. And let her know *she* was loved. Just the way *she* was.

Not because it would keep the peace, but because it felt like the right thing to do.

She opened her eyes, and lay slowly back on her bed, wrapping her arms about her stomach.

It was time for Avery to go home.

Late the next morning, Avery hung up from her dad.

He'd sounded…if not *over the moon* about his upcoming nuptials, about as close to as Phillip Maxwell Shaw ever got when not talking about the Dow Jones or the Yankees batting line-up.

She'd also discovered that he *knew*. He knew her mother still pined for him, had known for the past ten years that her feelings hadn't flagged, which was probably why he hadn't put out a cease and desist order the times she'd gone past the edge of reason.

Avery sank her face into her hands, letting the darkness behind her eyelids cool her thoughts.

Maybe the life lesson she'd been meant to learn from them *wasn't* that love was a perfect storm of emotional vertigo teetering on the precipice of destruction. Maybe it was just to be *honest* about it. Because if her mother and father had just had a candid conversation in the past ten years they could have saved themselves a hell of a lot of trouble. And *her*.

Her phone beeped. She breathed in a lungful of air, eyes refocusing.

You up for a swim? I can practically guarantee your survival.
Jonah.

Seeing his name was like an electric shock, shooting her from nonplussed to high alert. She'd wondered if the barrage of news, and the bright light of day, might dim her feelings. But if anything they'd taken on a new sharp-ness. A new veracity.

And the thought of going home, of saying goodbye, of never seeing him again, made her hurt. But she was going home. It was what happened after that that remained a big gloomy blur.

Her palms felt slick as she answered.

Meet you on the beach in ten.

She couldn't feel her feet as she made her way through the halls, through Reception, and outside.

She found Jonah leaning against his sleek black car, his naked torso gleaming in the shadows, his surfboard lean-ing beside him, Hull making circles in the grass beneath a palm tree before he sat with a *hurumph*.

Jonah looked up, took in her short white shorts, slinky black wraparound top, her strappy sandals. Her lack of a towel.

He pushed away from the car, his mouth kicking into a half-smile even as his eyes remained strangely flat. "I get that you're a city girl, but earrings?"

He looked so gorgeous. Her heart slammed against her ribs and she perched on his bumper to catch her breath.

Jonah joined her. Close enough to catch his scent, his warmth, far enough not to touch. As if he knew she was leaving. And how much she didn't want to.

She turned to find him looking back towards the Tropi-cana. "Jonah, I've booked my flight home."

Air filled his chest, his nostrils flaring, a frown darting across his brow before he looked down at his bare toes. Then finally, finally he looked her way, his grey eyes un-readable. His mouth so grim she could have been mistaken for thinking it had never learned to smile at all. "When?"

"Early this morning."

"No, when do you leave?"

"Oh." Her cheeks pinked. She felt so raw, so terrified by his reaction or lack thereof.

"Three days."

He breathed out. Nodded once. As if it was no surprise. And yet a world-weariness settled over him, adding a grey tinge to the golden halo that made him always seem more than a mere mortal. She could only hope that it was because he felt some fraction of what she felt for him. One way or the other, she'd soon find out.

"I'd like to come back. Soon." Deep breath. *Be honest.* "I'd like to come back to see you."

He didn't comment. Didn't even blink. A muscle ticcing once in his jaw as he looked across the road.

"Or maybe you'd like to come visit me."

She shrugged, as if it didn't matter either way. When really her heart was now desperately trying to take its leave of the space behind her ribs and jump into his hands and say, *Do with me as you please, because I'm all yours!*

"I can show you around Manhattan. I think you'd love the park. And Liberty Island is a pretty special place. I promise not to drag you around Saks.'

As the words spilled out of her mouth she even began to see how it might work. How a long-distance relationship was actually…not impossible. They both had the means.

They both just had to want it enough.

Her want was palpable, running about inside her with such speed she had to hug herself so it didn't escape. All that aching hope was what finally woke Pollyanna. She gave a yawning stretch, stood to attention, brushed the dust from her hands, about to say, *Right, let's get this thing done!* But before she could open her mouth, Jonah came to.

"Avery," he said, his voice ocean-deep. "This has been fun. But we both knew it was only going to last until it was time for you to go."

Avery uncurled her spine and sat up straight, all the better to breathe. "That was the plan, sure. But plans can change. I'm saying...I'd like the plan to change."

There, Avery thought, breathing out hard.

Jonah shot her a glance, so fleeting it brushed past her eyes and away, but long enough she caught the heat, the ache, the want. Then said, "Not going to happen."

"Why?"

"Because I have a job here, Avery. One that's been getting short shrift of late. I have ties here. Because I have responsibilities I'm not about to turn my back on. Because *this* is where I want to be."

Avery flinched as his voice rose. "I know that. I'm not asking you to *move*. Or give up anything. Or change who you are. Just to spend some time. With me."

The look he shot her told her he didn't believe her for a second. Been there, done that, lived to regret every second.

"Jonah—"

"Avery. Just stop," he said, exasperation ravaging the edges of his voice.

She shifted on the bumper bar till her knees bumped his, the scoot of heat nothing in the quagmire of frustration and fear riding her roughshod. "This," she said, "from the man who came over huffy when he thought I had intimated he might be parochial! The cove is wonderful. I give it that. But I've travelled. I've seen a hundred places equally gorgeous. So why are you *really* hiding out at the end of the earth?"

His expression was cool, his voice cooler, as he said, "I'm not hiding, Avery. I'm home."

She snorted. Real ladylike.

But at least it seemed to snap him from his shell. "I've tried it out there, Avery. It's not for me."

The urge to scoff again was gone before it ever took

hold once she realised—by *out there* he didn't mean Sydney. He meant *love*.

He'd put his heart *out there*, and had it sent spinning right on back. She wanted to tell him she wouldn't do that. Wouldn't leave him like his mother. Wouldn't pretend to feel something as his ex had. Wouldn't let him flounder while she got on with her life like his dad had done.

But by the stern set of his jaw she realised he wouldn't believe her.

No snorting then. Just a sudden constriction in her chest as she saw the raw honesty in Jonah's clear grey eyes. The determination. The conviction that this was no different. She was no different.

God, how she wanted to hit him! To thump his big chest till he got it. That for them summer could go on forever. They…both…just…had…to…want…it.

And then it hit her, like a smack to the back of the head. She might want it enough for the both of them. But—as proven by events on the other side of the planet—it would never be enough.

"This can't be it," she said, the words tearing from her throat.

"Honey," he said, and this time it felt so much like a real endearment she opened her eyes wider to halt the tears. He saw. Right through her, as always. But instead of doing what the twitch in his jaw told her he wanted to do—to run his thumb underneath her eye, to slide his big hand over her shoulder, to haul her in tight—he sniffed out a breath of frustration and ran two hands down his face. And said, "This summer has been a blast. But like every summer before it has to end. It's time for you to go home. And soon you'll look back and thank your lucky stars you did."

Avery shook her head, her fingers biting into the hot metal at her backside.

Not having Jonah in her life would *not* be better than having him in it. She hadn't needed to hear her mother say it to know *that* for sure. But he looked at her with such clarity, such resolution.

"How can you just switch off like that? Tell me. Because I really want to know how to make this feeling—" She slammed a closed fist against her ribs, the surface hurt nothing on the tight ball of pain inside. "How can you make it just go away?"

"Avery—"

"I'm serious. *Can* you turn it off? Just like that? Honestly?"

He looked at her. Right into her eyes. As tears of frustration finally spilled down her cheeks. He looked right into her eyes, not even a flicker of reaction to her pain. And he said, "I can."

Then he leaned over, wrapped an arm about her shoulders, kissed her on top of her head, lifted himself from the back of his car, grabbed his surfboard, and took off for the water at a jog.

CHAPTER ELEVEN

HE COULDN'T.

The night of the party Jonah had convinced himself that the only way not to feel like crap at being left was by doing the leaving himself. As if *that* was the common denominator of the shittiest times of his life; the fact that they had been out of his control.

Turned out it didn't matter a lick. Two days on, walking away from Avery still bit. Like a shark bite, a great chunk of him missing, the wound exposed to the salty air.

"Storm's a coming."

"What?"

Tim backed up to the office door, two hands raised in surrender. "Nora said you were in a snit. I said, 'More than usual?' She said, 'Go poke the bear and you'll find out.'"

Jonah pinned his second in charge with a flat stare. "Consider me poked."

Tim lolloped into the office and sat. "Want to talk about it?"

"I'll give you one guess."

"Avery," Tim said, nodding sadly.

Right guess, wrong answer. Knowing Tim well enough to know the only way out of this was through, Jonah ran two hands over his face and turned his chair to look out over the water. The sun glinted so fiercely through a mass of gathering grey clouds he had to squint.

"She's really leaving, huh?" Tim asked.

A muscle twitched in Jonah's cheek. "You'll find that's what holidaymakers do. Keeps the tourist dollars spinning. Pays your wage and mine."

A pause from Tim. Then, "She's been doing the rounds of the entire town. Saying goodbye. And leaving little gifts." Tim held up his hand, a plaited friendship bracelet circling his arm. "It matches Roger's."

"Lucky Roger."

"What did she leave you?"

The knowledge that he'd been knocked around more times than he could count in his thirty-odd years on earth and hadn't learned a damn thing.

Jonah pushed himself to standing and grabbed his keys from the fish hook by the door. "I have to go. Appointment. Tell Nora to transfer calls to my mobile."

Tim saluted. "Aye-aye, Cap'n."

Jonah jogged through the offices. His staff were smart enough to leave him be.

Truth was he did have an appointment; one he'd made a week before. Once outside and at the Monaro, as he pressed the remote lock Hull apparated from nowhere to appear at his heels, his liquid eyes quietly sad, as if he knew what he was in for.

When the sorry truth was he was probably pining for Avery. Whole damn east coast was apparently pining for Avery.

Jonah clicked his fingers and Hull jumped in the back of the car. Jonah gunned the engine, the wild rumble of the muscle car matching his mood to perfection. He wound down the windows, thumbed the buttons till he found a song on the radio that had a hope in hell of numbing his mind. Then he set off for the vet.

For big Hull was getting the snip.

He'd be better off castrated. For one thing he could go

through life never again noticing the Petunias of the world. No more urges that were as helpful as a hole in the head.

For half a second Jonah was envious. An operation might be pushing it, but he'd take a pill if it meant ridding himself of the ache behind his ribs that refused to let up.

With a rumble of gears, he hit the freeway leading down the coast towards the cove.

Towards Avery. Yeah, she was still out there somewhere— lazing on the beach, drinking those coconutty things she couldn't get enough of, wearing some delectable excuse for swimwear, laughing in that loose sexy way of hers—

She hadn't been laughing, or smiling, when he'd last seen her. He'd been harsh. He'd had to. Even as she'd floated the idea to keep it going, he'd felt the same pull so strongly it had threatened to take him under. Because what he'd had with her was better than anything he'd ever had with another human being in the entire history of his life on earth.

But he'd had to make a clean break.

He lifted a hand to shield his face from the burning sun shining through the driver's side window, and pulled into the fast lane to overtake a semi-trailer. The road shook beneath him, rattling his teeth.

After his mother left, his childhood had been waylaid by waiting for the other shoe to drop. By the expectation that more bad things were to come. And they had, when his father had died. He'd realised too late that waiting for it to happen hadn't made it any easier. So with Rach, instead of waiting he'd leapt in, held on tighter. Not because *her* leaving had been that much of a shock—but because he was looking for a connection, *any* connection, something to prove he was more than a dandelion seed caught on the wind.

Half an hour later he pulled up at the shack. Jogging up the steps, he went inside to grab Hull's new lead, copies of the paperwork he'd recently filled out to register Hull with the local council as his dog, and Hull's favourite chew toy.

And there, right in the middle of his sun-drenched entryway, he stopped dead. Looked around. And felt Avery everywhere. He felt her in the tilt of his kitchen chair, better angled to the sun. Felt her in the throw rug draped over his couch, the one she wrapped about her feet that always got cold at night.

He stared at Hull's chew toy in his hand; Avery had ordered it online—a rubber hot dog in Yankees colours.

Poor Hull who was about to get the snip. Who'd never again have the chance to find himself a girl. The *right* girl.

Jonah was running back to the car when the first raindrops hit.

Only to find Hull was gone.

"Jonah! Excellent. You staying?" Claudia asked as she saw Jonah taking the front steps of the Tropicana two at a time.

"Where?"

"Here! Storm's a coming, my friend. A big one!" Claude poked her hand outside, captured a few stray raindrops in her palm. "Can't hate a storm when it brings a town's worth of guests through my front door to use my cellar as a safe area! Would it be poor form to hand out brochures with the water?"

He shook his head. "Claude, I'm looking for Hull."

"Not here. Why?"

"Doesn't matter." Jonah rocked on his feet; half of him keen to look for Hull, the other half somewhat stuck. "Everyone's down in the cellar?"

"Everyone who's anyone. I'm thinking it's the perfect chance to show off what the Tropicana Nights is all about."

"Natural disaster management?"

"Fun," she glowered. "Submarine theme, perhaps.

Caveman, maybe. Mum and Dad had an awesome collection of faux animal skins back in the day."

A themed bunker, Jonah thought. *Heaven help them all.* And then his thoughts shifted back to where they'd been moments before. Where they constantly strayed.

He couldn't ask—he didn't have the right after what he'd done—but it came out anyway. "Avery there already?"

Claude shot him a flat stare. "She's gone, Jonah. No thanks to you."

"Gone where?"

"Gone gone. Back to the U. S. of A. To the bright lights and freezing winters and her suffocating mother and neglectful father. I thought we had her this time. That our beautiful butterfly had finally realised she had wings. But no. Flight to JFK leaves in…fifteen minutes. Or left fifteen minutes ago. Not sure which."

Time slowed, then came to a screeching halt. Avery was gone. Out of his life for good. As the full realisation of all that meant wrapped about him like a dark wet cloak, Jonah was amazed he could find his voice at all. "But she wasn't due to leave for a couple of days."

"Time to get back to *real life,*" Claudia said, taking a moment to glare at him between happily ticking off the list on her clipboard. "I tried to make her stay despite it, but I wasn't the one who could."

"Meaning?"

"There's a *storm* a coming. I don't have time for all this. Use that brain in that pretty little head of yours and think!"

Think he did. So hard he near burst a blood vessel.

Why? Why was he making himself feel like crap when he didn't need to? Fear she'd some day make him feel like crap and he wanted to get there first? Life had taught him some hard lessons. Some at a pretty early age. And there was no certainty there wouldn't be more hard lessons to come.

Didn't mean he couldn't buck the system. He'd done it

before, in dragging himself up by his bootstraps. He could do it again. Damn well *should* do it again, if that was what it took to have the life he wanted. To be happy.

"Don't worry about Hull," Claudia said, drawing him out of the throbbing quagmire inside his head. "He'll have found a safe haven somewhere hiding out from the storm. Dogs are smart."

"What storm?"

"Storm!" she said, taking him by the cheeks and turning his face to look through the huge front doors across the street and over the water where grey clouds swarmed like an invasion from the skies.

Where the hell had that come from? How had he not known? He owned a fleet of boats, for heaven's sake. Phone already at his ear, he called Charter North. "Nora. Get Tim to—"

Jonah listened with half an ear as he pounded down the front stairs, his eyes on the menacing clouds overhead. Turned out Tim had somehow known he might not be quite on his game and had done all that had to be done. Good man. The second he next saw him the guy was getting a promotion.

Jonah hung up and looked to the skies. And his heart imploded on the spot.

Avery was flying into that?

"If you see Hull," he called out, his voice sounding as if it were coming from the bottom of a well, "get him under cover. Don't dress him up in any way, shape or form."

"Count on it!" Claudia called back. "Where are you going?"

"To bring our girl home."

"'Atta boy!" she said, then shut the front door.

Hull was strong. Hull was smart. He'd be somewhere dry, waiting out the wet. Just as Jonah had planned to wait out the heartache of letting Avery go.

Only the storm in his head, in his heart, was of his own making. And as he set off to rescue his girl, he did so with a slice of fear cutting through him the likes of which he'd never felt. And hope.

He reached his car right as raindrops hit the road with fat slaps, and when the skies opened and dumped their contents on the cove he was already headed to the airport.

Avery sat in the cab, which had been stuck in the same spot for over an hour, the rain outside lashing the windows.

"Car accident," the cabbie said.

"Mmm?"

"Radio's saying car accident. Hasn't rained here for weeks. Oil on the road gets slick. Accidents happen." He leant forward to peer through the rain-hammered window and up into the grey skies. "Any luck your flight's been cancelled."

When he realised Avery wasn't in a chatty mood, he shrugged and went back to his phone.

She didn't mind. The shushing of the rain was a background of white noise against her disorderly thoughts.

She'd been thinking about moving, actually. Farther down the island. It would be healthy to keep some of the distance the trip had given her from her family.

Her apartment was a sublet, after all. Her job freelance too, despite numerous headhunters desperate to secure her. Even her house plants were fake. Heck, she'd only bought a one-way ticket on her holiday, ambivalence stopping her from even committing to when she might return.

She'd felt holier than thou that Jonah couldn't commit to a dog? She'd never even committed to her life.

Why not some real distance? she thought, shifting her thoughts. In San Diego the weather was spectacular. And she did have a huge bikini collection she'd hate to see go to waste.

No. Not San Diego. Too much blue sky, too much sea air, too many reminders of here.

Head thunking against the head rest, Avery thought back to that afternoon in the hammock, blithely admitting to herself that she'd sure miss Jonah when she left. As if admitting she cared meant it was somehow in her control. But it never had been. From the moment he'd yanked her out of the ocean, he was doomed to invade her heart. And now that he'd retreated, her poor abandoned heart hurt like a thousand paper cuts.

What she wouldn't do to have her hands around his neck right about then. Squeezing hard. Then softening, sliding over his throat, the rasp of his stubble against her soft palms…

She sat up straight and shook her head.

A fresh start was what she needed. A clear head with which to start her own life, one not all tied up in her mother's troubles, her father's impending nuptials, or her own heartache.

She ran both hands over her eyes that felt gritty with lack of sleep.

Yep. When she got home changes would be made. She'd soak in the moments as they happened. Do work that truly satisfied. Give her mother a daughter's love, and hold the rest of herself back so that there was something left over. Enough that she could offer it to somebody else. Somebody she loved who loved her back.

Because she'd learned all too well these past weeks that home wasn't where you laid your hat; it was whose hat lay next to yours. Those mornings waking up in Jonah's bed—to find him breathing softly, his deep grey eyes drinking her in as if she was the most beautiful thing he'd ever seen—were the most real, alive moments of her life.

A half life wasn't enough for her any more. She had to be thankful for that.

A crack of thunder split the air, rocking the cab with it. "Whoa," said the cabbie with nervous laughter.

But Avery's mind was elsewhere. Flittering through the past few weeks, to the tentative way she and Jonah had begun, circling one another like dogs who'd been kicked in the teeth by love their whole lives. How they'd come together with such flash and fire, only to blithely pretend that it was everyday. That it was normal. That they could go about their daily lives afterwards.

She couldn't. Being with Jonah had pried her open, forced her to reach deep inside and grab for what she wanted. Made her feel deeply, broadly, inside outside upside down and so thoroughly there was no going back. Not even if she wanted to.

And she didn't.

She didn't want to go back at all.

She wanted Jonah. And Hull. And the cove. She wanted that life. And the Tropicana Nights. And to help Claude. And heat and sunshine. And storms that looked as if they could rip trees from the ground. She wanted passion and light and life. Even if it was dangerous. Even if it was hard.

It was her best life. Her best moments. Her happiest self. But none of that existed without him. Which was where she came full circle yet again.

Not that she'd out and out *told* him that she loved him. She'd hinted. She'd hoped he might notice and make the first move into forever.

Jonah whose mother had left him behind. Jonah whose father had never had time for him.

"Here we go," the taxi driver said, warming up the engine once more.

When they started towards the airport, Avery looked back in panic. "Wait."

"Wait what?"

"Can we please turn around?"

"Not go to the airport?"

She shook her head. "Crescent Cove," she shouted over the sound of the rain now pelting against the car from all angles. "Whatever your fare ends up being, I'll double it."

She felt the car accelerate beneath her backside, and her heart rate rose to match.

Her parents had never been fully honest with one another, which had led to ten years of suffering. No matter what else she got wrong in her life, she'd not make *that* mistake.

She was going to find Jonah, and this time she was going to tell him how she felt.

And if Jonah was so sure he didn't feel the same way he'd just have to tell her he didn't love her back. Right to her face.

"I have to call Jonah," Avery said, panting as she trudged inside the Tropicana Nights with her sopping-wet luggage in tow. She peeled a few random leaves from her skin, and wiped away as much sand as she could.

The weather was wild out there. So much so she knew the only reason the driver had been stupid enough to keep going was the double fare she'd promised at the end of it.

Claude—wearing a moth-eaten ancient faux bear-skin over her head and holding what looked mighty like a cavegirl club—quickly shut the door behind them. "He went looking for you."

Avery stopped wringing water from her hair and looked at Claude, who was by then trying to drag her into the resort. "For me? Why?"

Claude looked at her as if she were nuts. Then when Avery continued to be daft said, "Because the woman he loves was about to fly away and out of his life? The man might be stubborn as an ass, but he's not stupid."

"He told you he *loved* me?"

Avery took a step back towards the door before Claude took her by the upper arms and looked her dead in the eye. "Storm, Avery. Everything else can wait."

She looked over Claude's shoulder to the empty foyer beyond. The lights were low, the place dark as the sun was completely blocked out by the storm. "Will you be okay?"

"We'll be fine. She's a tough old place. Strong. We're a safety point," Claude said. "Wine cellar, foods storage bunkers. Enough room to fit a hundred-odd people underground."

Avery gave her a hug and without further ado walked out into the storm.

Her clothes slapped against her limbs and the sand in the swirling winds bit at her skin. The double row of palm trees lining the beach path were swaying back and forth with such ferocity it was amazing they weren't uprooted.

She was halfway down the stairs before she realised the cab had gone.

Dammit.

Dragging her slippery hair out of her face, she took two more steps down to the path, looked up the deserted beach and down, before making to turn around, go inside. To dry out her phone. To call—

Which was when she saw a figure huddled under a tree in the front yard of a cottage overlooking the beach. A wet, bedraggled, speckled four-legged figure.

"Hull?" she called. The dog glanced up then sank deeper against the tree. She called louder this time. "Hull! Come on, boy. Come inside!"

But Hull just sat there, in the squall. This dog who *hated* water. What was he doing out in this craziness?

Lifting the back of her shirt over her head, she jogged down the steps, down the footpath, and into the front yard, slowing in case Hull was hurt. In case the hurt made him lash out instead of accepting comfort. She knew his owner, after all.

"Come on, boy," she said, sliding her arm around his wet neck. He whimpered up at her, his tail giving a double beat against the sodden ground. But he dug his heels in and bayed up at the window of the house whose yard he was camped in where the curtains flickered ominously.

When she realised he had no intention of moving, Avery sat down next to him, the shade of the tree giving them no respite at all from the onslaught. Soon she was soaked through to the skin. A little later she began to shiver.

"What are we doing here, Hull?" she asked, when the rain got so hard she could no longer see the beach at all.

He whimpered and turned to look forlornly up at the house outside which they'd camped. A small, white, flat-fronted brick cabin, with a picture of a familiar dog in an oval frame on the front door.

"No, Hull. Seriously?"

A storm was raging about them, and here Hull sat, crooning outside Petunia's house, pining for his love.

"Where did you come from, kid?" she asked, hugging him tighter. "I can't even get your owner to admit he cares for me at all."

Hull gave Avery's hand a single lick. She ran her fingers down his wet snout. And there they sat, getting drenched, ducking out of the way of the occasional falling branch, watching in bemused silence as lawn furniture went tumbling down the street. Till Avery began to fear for more than her poor heart.

Yet it all faded away when she heard the throaty growl of Jonah's car before she saw it come around the bend. She waved, and the car pulled to a halt in the middle of the street, the wheels spinning as he ground to a sudden sodden halt. It screeched into Reverse, backed up, then mounted the kerb as it pulled up across the driveway.

As Jonah leapt from the car Avery pulled herself to standing, her legs frozen solid. She tripped as she tried to walk, her legs cramped into a bend.

Jonah was there to catch her.

"Jonah," she said, wanting to tell him, to ask him, to show him…

But then she was in his arms and he was kissing her and bliss sank through her limbs. He kissed her as if his life depended upon it. As if she were his breath, his blood, his everything.

When he pulled back, he drew her into his chest and rested his chin atop her head. They both breathed heavily, rain thundering down upon them, but the sound of his heart was the only thing she heard.

When she looked up, he held her face between his hands. Emotion stormed across her eyes, too deep, too violent to catch.

"I found your dog."

"I see that," he said and his eyes smiled as they roved over her face, raking in every inch as if making sure she was really real.

"I rescued him, in fact."

"You rescued him? From a little rain?"

She slapped his chest, her hand bouncing off the hard planes before settling there, her nails scraping his wet T-shirt, her heart kicking against her ribs. "From being sued by a crazy woman."

Jonah's brow furrowed. Avery tilted her head towards the cottage. "Hull's girl lives here."

Jonah's eyes finally left hers to take in the front door with its picture of a tiny, near bald, shivering scrap of flesh that was barely rat, much less a dog. Jonah's eyes swung back to her, and he used both hands, both big, warm, rough hands, to gently peel the lank hair from her cheeks.

When Avery began to shiver harder it had nothing to

do with being thoroughly drenched. And as his hands roved down her arms, and up again, she was heading very quickly from lusciously warm to scorching hot.

But knowing he'd need encouragement, a place to feel safe to tell her what she needed to hear, Avery nudged. "Is that why you were driving around? You were worried about Hull in the rain and all?"

Jonah breathed deep through his nose, his clear grey eyes glinting. "I trusted he'd take care of himself. You, on the other hand—"

"What about me?" she said, rearing back. Not far, though. Enough to show her chagrin while still being plastered well and truly against him. "I'm perfectly capable of taking care of myself."

"I know. You're plenty tough, Avery Shaw. And yet I can't seem to fight the urge to look after you. In fact, I'm done. Done fighting it. Done fighting how I feel about you."

Avery swallowed hard while her belly flipped and started singing the Hallelujah chorus.

"Avery, I barely got halfway to the airport when I heard there was an accident. The thought that it might have been you, that you might be hurt—there are no words to explain how that felt. I called Claude. And she said you were here. And I can't possibly explain the relief."

Try, she thought. "Why were you going to the airport?"

"To *find* you, woman. To haul you back here. Or, hell, to go with you, or ask if you'd care to try living transcontinentally, if that's what you wanted. So long as you were where you belong. With me."

"You'd leave the cove? For me?"

"Not for you, Miss Shaw. With you... If it meant being able to do this—" he kissed the corner of her mouth "—and this—" he kissed the other corner "—and also this—" he placed his mouth over hers with infinite gentleness, infinite subtlety, until Avery felt as if the only thing holding her cells together were his touch.

When she shivered so hard her teeth rattled, Jonah scooped her up and deposited her in the back seat of his car. He joined her there. The curtains in the cottage continued to flicker, yet Hull kept up his vigil beneath the tree.

In the dry hollow of the car, Avery turned to face Jonah. Water glistened in his gorgeous curls, turned his lashes into dark spiky clumps, and gave his lips a seductive sheen that made her clench in deep-down places.

Raindrops still sluiced down her nose, running in rivulets beneath her now-muddy clothes. She was bedraggled. And yet he didn't seem to mind. In fact he was looking at her as if she were his moon and stars.

And then he had to go and completely tear her apart by saying, "I'm in love with you, Avery Shaw. And even if you live on the other side of the world, I'm going to keep on loving you. And if you think that's something you can live with, then we have some figuring out to do."

Could she live with it? With being loved by this man? This man who made her feel so much she couldn't contain it?

She threw herself at him so thoroughly she banged her knee, rocking the car. But pain was way in the background beneath the million other far more wonderful sensations pelting her all over as she kissed the man she loved for all that she was worth.

"I'm assuming this means you're all in favour?" he asked, when he came up for air.

"I love you. I love you, I love you, I love you!" she said. Laughing, shouting, fogging up the windows with all that beautiful, *beautiful* kissing.

The storm disappeared as quickly as it had come.

When Avery and Jonah left the cocoon of the car—

having broken several public indecency laws—they managed to encourage poor Hull away, and the three of them
made their way over to the beach to check out the damage only to find the cove looking as if nothing had happened at all.

But everything had happened.

Jonah took Avery's hand and pulled her down onto a
patch of sand in the shade of the palms. Her cheeks hurt
from smiling and with a sigh she looked out over the waves
of the Pacific. It was a completely different ocean from
the one back home, and yet it didn't feel so far from everything at all. Because everything she wanted more than
anything else was right here.

EPILOGUE

AVERY STOOD OUTSIDE the Tropicana Nights, eyes closed, arms outstretched, soaking up the blissful warmth that made this part of the world so famous.

Jonah grunted behind her as he dragged her bags out of the car. She had more luggage this time; she was staying longer, after all. Forever, in fact.

"Avery!" Claude said, running down the stairs, her Tropicana Nights uniform shirt brighter than the sun, her clipboard flapping at her side, Hull at her ankles.

"God, am I glad to have you back! This dog of yours pined the entire month you were gone."

Hull came bounding up, spry as a puppy, with a big new collar around his neck. Avery checked the label—a doggy bone with his name engraved into the front. On the back, *Property of Jonah North.*

"Want one?" Claude said low enough for only her to hear with a grin when Avery motioned to the tag. "How was your holiday?" she added, this time for all to hear. "Did I say how glad I am you're back? Did Jonah grumble the whole time?"

Yeah, Jonah had grumbled, Avery thought, turning to watch him crouch to take his dog—*their* dog—in a huge cuddle. Hull's tongue lolled out of his mouth as Jonah boxed him about the ears, and when Jonah laughed the dog wagged his tail so hard he near dented the car.

New York was so grey, Jonah had noted, and too cold, too many people, air so thick you could choke on it, the Hudson a poor substitute for the Pacific Ocean. But then again she found his particular brand of manly grumpiness kind of hot, so she was all good.

Also, he'd completely charmed her mother, who seemed to have come blinking into the light now that her father had truly moved on. Jonah had kept toe to toe with her dad, talking baseball stats as if he were born to it. As for her father's new fiancée, she'd turned out to be pretty nice. It had been no shock when half her friends fell in lust with Jonah on the spot, and he'd let her take him to shows, and to all the tourist traps, and when they'd stayed at the top of the Empire State Building for hours it had been his idea.

Then the Yankees won their first three exhibition games three out of three, which pretty much trumped the rest.

"The place is looking great, Claude."

"Isn't it?" She looked up at the freshly whitewashed facade, gleaming in the sunlight.

"We heard there were more storms while we were away."

"Mere rain. Though it gave me the chance to do a vampire theme party in the bunker. I sent Luke the link to the blog post with all the photos. I've yet to hear back."

"So the stay of execution is still in play?"

"He's given me a year. So the work's only just begun!"

"I love work. Bring on the work." Knowing how close Claude had come to losing her business, her home, she'd forced Claude to hire her without pay—she had a trust fund after all, and no longer any compunction about using it. Not for such a good cause.

"The press we had after the party was unbelievable, and the website guy you set me up with is awesome, and we have bookings flying in. This place is going to be as amazing as it was in its heyday."

"More amazing! Is Luke back to help?"

Claudia frowned so hard her cheeks pinked up in an instant. "Forget about Luke. All we have to concern ourselves with is making this resort the premier family destination in Far North Queensland."

"That's the spirit."

"Now, I've ordered a whole bunch of uniforms in your size—"

"Oh, not necessary, really. I've brought so many great clothes—"

"Nonsense. You are one of the team now. Uniform's a must. All about the brand."

Avery grimaced at Jonah, who grinned back, and even the thought of spending her working hours in Hawaiian print shirts and polyester capris couldn't dampen her spirits. Because, oh, she loved that smile. And the man behind it. The way those deep grey eyes of his saw through her, right to the most vulnerable heart of her, and loved her in a way she'd never dared hope she could be.

"Claude," Jonah called, his voice deep with warning.

Claudia looked over Avery's shoulder at him. "Hmm?"

"Leave the woman alone. The last time she tried to do anything strenuous while dopey with jet lag she nearly drowned."

"I did no such thing," Avery started. "I'm—"

"An excellent swimmer," Jonah joined in. "Yeah, I know."

"Fine, yes, of course!" Claudia said, backing up. She clicked her fingers at Cyrus.

The lanky kid grabbed a trolley and ambled over to Jonah's car, heaving the bags into place. Cheek twitching, Jonah dragged them all off again and set about doing it right.

"Are you sure you're right to stay here?" Claudia asked as both women watched Jonah at work, arm muscles bunching, teeth gritting, the hem of his T-shirt lifting to showcase the most stunning set of abs ever created.

"Of course!" Avery said nice and loud. "Wasn't it you who said we have a lot of work to do?"

"Yeah, right," Claude muttered. "I give it a week before you're living at his place with that huge dog of his sleeping on your feet."

"Yeah," Avery said with a grin. Mention in passing the spotting of a man-eating spider in her room perhaps, and he'd turn up and throw her over his shoulder and whisk her away to his castle in the forest like her own personal knight. "I can't wait."

Claude scrunched up her nose. "Each to their own."

Claude grabbed one arm of the trolley and dragged it and Cyrus along the path around the side of the resort to settle Avery back home.

Home.

Sea air tickled Avery's nose, heat poured and prickled all over her skin. She watched Jonah lift his face to the sky, the Queensland sun glowing against his golden-brown skin, infusing him with life.

Yeah, her guy might have wowed 'em in New York City, but he wasn't built for city living. He was built for this place. This raw, majestic, lovely, warm place. Lucky for them she could handle living in paradise.

Lucky for Avery, Jonah was also built for loving her.

Sensing he was being watched, he tipped his head to look at her. All dark curls and strong jaw, might and muscle and heat and hotness. And hers.

Feeling like she was sixteen all over again, full of hope and love and zeal, Avery ran and jumped into his arms. He caught her, swung her around, and held her tight as his lips met hers in a kiss that sank through her like melted butter.

"I love you, Jonah North, and don't you ever forget it."

"Yeah," he said, his arms wrapped about her tugging

her tighter still. "Couldn't if I tried. Now, come on, princess, time to get you to bed."

"Feisty."

"Insurance. I was serious about you getting some sleep after last time. I wouldn't put it past you to get it in your head to try parasailing for the first time. Hell, I might even strap you into bed so you don't do yourself damage."

"Extra spicy feisty." The effect of her sass was dampened when the last word was swallowed by a massive yawn.

As they walked through Reception Avery noticed at the edge of her mind that the place was busier than the last time she was there. Not bustling, but better.

Isis gave her a cheery wave. She waved back before her mind focused in on more important things, like the fact that Jonah's hand had moved down her waist until his fingers were at her hip.

Cyrus was leaving the Tiki Suite as they arrived. Yawning again, she fished through her wallet for a tip, came up with a twenty and tucked it into Cyrus's pocket, then trudged to the centre of the room and fell back on the bed with a thud.

Through the slits of her eyes she saw Jonah glare at Cyrus to make him leave. Which he did. Jonah locked the door behind him.

"That kid has a thing for you," Jonah said, thumb jerking at the door.

"I know. It's sweet."

Jonah turned slowly to stare at her, his eyes flat. "Honestly, how did you survive twenty-six years on that island without getting nabbed?"

"Street smarts. And the deep-down knowledge that I'd only ever get nabbed if the right man did the nabbing."

"Oh, yeah?" Jonah said, sliding his hands into his pockets even as he edged her way.

She lifted her weary self up onto her elbows as she was suddenly not so weary after all. "A handsome man, he'd be. A little full of himself, but understandably so." Her eyes roved down his torso, his long, strong legs to his feet, which were nudging off his shoes. "A successful man too. Helicopter an absolute must. As is..." her wandering gaze landed on the impressive bulge in his jeans "...heft."

"Heft?" he coughed out, laughing in that deep, delicious *huh-huh-huh* way that made her spine tingle and then some.

"Cerebral heft. Emotional heft. General...heft."

Jonah and his heft left a mighty dent in the mattress as he lowered himself over her, a halo of sunlight around his gorgeous curls. His dark eyes on her mouth. His knee sliding between hers and up, and up.

"Whoever this perfect man is, he can shove off, because he's too damn late. From the moment I pulled you out of the water, I owned you, Avery Shaw. You're mine—" he punctuated that one with a kiss, a long, slow, hot, bone-melting kiss "—all mine."

"Okay!" she said, sliding her arms around his neck to pull him down for more.

Jet lag be damned. The only drowning she planned to do that day and every day forth was in bliss. Pure, unadulterated bliss. Starting right now.

Because saying Yes—capital *Y* intended—had never felt more right.

* * * * *

Don't miss Claudia's story next month!
THE HEAT OF THE NIGHT by Amy Andrews
is available next month—
only in Harlequin KISS on eBook!

Mills & Boon® Hardback
July 2014

ROMANCE

Christakis's Rebellious Wife	Lynne Graham
At No Man's Command	Melanie Milburne
Carrying the Sheikh's Heir	Lynn Raye Harris
Bound by the Italian's Contract	Janette Kenny
Dante's Unexpected Legacy	Catherine George
A Deal with Demakis	Tara Pammi
The Ultimate Playboy	Maya Blake
Socialite's Gamble	Michelle Conder
Her Hottest Summer Yet	Ally Blake
Who's Afraid of the Big Bad Boss?	Nina Harrington
If Only...	Tanya Wright
Only the Brave Try Ballet	Stefanie London
Her Irresistible Protector	Michelle Douglas
The Maverick Millionaire	Alison Roberts
The Return of the Rebel	Jennifer Faye
The Tycoon and the Wedding Planner	Kandy Shepherd
The Accidental Daddy	Meredith Webber
Pregnant with the Soldier's Son	Amy Ruttan

MEDICAL

200 Harley Street: The Shameless Maverick	Louisa George
200 Harley Street: The Tortured Hero	Amy Andrews
A Home for the Hot-Shot Doc	Dianne Drake
A Doctor's Confession	Dianne Drake

Mills & Boon® Large Print

July 2014

ROMANCE

A Prize Beyond Jewels	Carole Mortimer
A Queen for the Taking?	Kate Hewitt
Pretender to the Throne	Maisey Yates
An Exception to His Rule	Lindsay Armstrong
The Sheikh's Last Seduction	Jennie Lucas
Enthralled by Moretti	Cathy Williams
The Woman Sent to Tame Him	Victoria Parker
The Plus-One Agreement	Charlotte Phillips
Awakened By His Touch	Nikki Logan
Road Trip with the Eligible Bachelor	Michelle Douglas
Safe in the Tycoon's Arms	Jennifer Faye

HISTORICAL

The Fall of a Saint	Christine Merrill
At the Highwayman's Pleasure	Sarah Mallory
Mishap Marriage	Helen Dickson
Secrets at Court	Blythe Gifford
The Rebel Captain's Royalist Bride	Anne Herries

MEDICAL

Her Hard to Resist Husband	Tina Beckett
The Rebel Doc Who Stole Her Heart	Susan Carlisle
From Duty to Daddy	Sue MacKay
Changed by His Son's Smile	Robin Gianna
Mr Right All Along	Jennifer Taylor
Her Miracle Twins	Margaret Barker

ROMANCE

Zarif's Convenient Queen	Lynne Graham
Uncovering Her Nine Month Secret	Jennie Lucas
His Forbidden Diamond	Susan Stephens
Undone by the Sultan's Touch	Caitlin Crews
The Argentinian's Demand	Cathy Williams
Taming the Notorious Sicilian	Michelle Smart
The Ultimate Seduction	Dani Collins
Billionaire's Secret	Chantelle Shaw
The Heat of the Night	Amy Andrews
The Morning After the Night Before	Nikki Logan
Here Comes the Bridesmaid	Avril Tremayne
How to Bag a Billionaire	Nina Milne
The Rebel and the Heiress	Michelle Douglas
Not Just a Convenient Marriage	Lucy Gordon
A Groom Worth Waiting For	Sophie Pembroke
Crown Prince, Pregnant Bride	Kate Hardy
Daring to Date Her Boss	Joanna Neil
A Doctor to Heal Her Heart	Annie Claydon

MEDICAL

Tempted by Her Boss	Scarlet Wilson
His Girl From Nowhere	Tina Beckett
Falling For Dr Dimitriou	Anne Fraser
Return of Dr Irresistible	Amalie Berlin

Mills & Boon® Large Print

August 2014

ROMANCE

HISTORICAL

MEDICAL

Discover more romance at

www.millsandboon.co.uk

- ❤ WIN great prizes in our exclusive competitions
- ❤ BUY new titles before they hit the shops
- ❤ BROWSE new books and REVIEW your favourites
- ❤ SAVE on new books with the Mills & Boon® Bookclub™
- ❤ DISCOVER new authors

PLUS, to chat about your favourite reads, get the latest news and find special offers:

- Find us on facebook.com/millsandboon
- Follow us on twitter.com/millsandboonuk
- ❤ Sign up to our newsletter at millsandboon.co.uk